# MY BIG FAT
# ZOMBIE
# GOLDFISH

D0386254

# MY BIG FAT ZOMBIE GOLDFISH

## MO O'HARA

## ILLUSTRATED BY MAREK JAGUCKI

SQUARE
FISH
FEIWEL AND FRIENDS
NEW YORK

SQUARE
FISH

An imprint of Macmillan Publishing Group, LLC
120 Broadway
New York, NY 10271
mackids.com

MY BIG FAT ZOMBIE GOLDFISH. Text copyright © 2013 by Mo O'Hara.
Illustrations copyright © 2013 by Marek Jagucki.
All rights reserved. Printed in the United States of America by
LSC Communications, Harrisonburg, Virginia.

Square Fish and the Square Fish logo are trademarks of Macmillan and
are used by Feiwel and Friends under license from Macmillan.

Square Fish books may be purchased for business or promotional use.
For information on bulk purchases, please contact
the Macmillan Corporate and Premium Sales Department at
(800) 221-7945 x5442 or by email at specialmarkets@macmillan.com.

A CIP catalogue record for this book is available from the British Library
ISBN 978-1-250-05215-5 (paperback) / 978-1-250-04241-5 (ebook)

Originally published in the UK by Macmillan Children's Books,
a division of Macmillan Publishers Limited.
First published in the United States by Feiwel and Friends
First Square Fish Edition 2014
Square Fish logo designed by Filomena Tuosto

23  25  27  29  30  28  26  24  22

AR: 4.8

*To my super-supportive family—Guy, Daniel, Charlotte, my mom and dad, JoAnne, and of course my big brother, who's grown up to be one of the least evil things I can imagine being—a bookseller*

# A FRANKLY SHOCKING TALE

# CHAPTER 1

# THE EVIL SCIENTIST

Yesterday my big brother, Mark, turned into
a real-life actual **EVIL SCIENTIST**. I mean, he
always was mostly evil anyway—you know,
knocking me down things or over things, locking
me in things or out of things, squashing me
under things or between things, that kind of
mostly evil stuff. But lately he's slid up the evil
scale from "mostly evil" to "nearly totally evil."
It started with the way he talked.

"Hey! Tom!" he shouted. "Remote! Now!"

Mark spoke in short words, like his brain had
shrunk or something. He grabbed the remote and
kicked my foot away. "Moron," he mumbled.

My best friend, Pradeep, who lives next door,
says that "moron" is a big-brother word for little
brothers. His brother, Sanj, who's also mostly
evil, calls him that too. Luckily Sanj is away
at boarding school though, so he can only be
mostly evil to Pradeep during school vacations.

I told my mom about Mark going more evil,
but Mom said it's just that Mark is "home-
moanal." Which I think is why he's moaning

at home a lot. She said he can't help acting evil (well, she didn't say evil exactly, but she should have). She said it's because he has lots of "home-moans" racing around his body.

Just when I thought Mark couldn't get worse, Granny and Grandad got him a chemistry set for his birthday. It came in a huge box with big official writing on the front that read:

WARNING! Only for use by children over twelve years old. To be used solely under the supervision of adults.

While I was reading the box, Mark thwacked my head from behind.

"Don't touch this—got it?" he said.

I walked away rubbing my head. Mostly because it hurt, but also to get my head out of the way in case he decided to thwack me again.

He took out a white scientist coat and looked at all the stuff inside the box. There were bottles and test tubes and cups and little stirring things, all made of glass. Real breakable glass! Mom looked at the chemistry set and leaned over to me.

"Maybe you shouldn't touch it, dear. It looks like an accident waiting to happen," she said.

YEAH, I'VE GOT A FEW MINUTES BEFORE THAT ACCIDENT I'M GONNA CAUSE. I CAN WAIT.

Mark put on the coat and turned around. He folded up the collar, shoved his hands in the pockets and let a creepy smile spread over his face. And you know that squirmy, prickly feeling you get when you let a millipede crawl on your arm? I had that feeling, but in my stomach.

Mark had turned into an **EVIL SCIENTIST**. But I didn't know how evil he could be until he came home the next day with the goldfish.

# CHAPTER 2
# A FISH IN A BAG

Now, we'd had goldfish before. We won them at a church fair by throwing ping-pong balls into the little bowls they were swimming in. They didn't live very long though. Mom said it was because the fish all had concussions from being hit on the head with the ping-pong balls.

I had a concussion once when I was four, after I accidentally ran into the front door that Mark *accidentally* slammed shut just as he *accidentally* yelled, "Run, Tom, run." That was back when he was just mostly evil.

I remember the doctor shining a tiny flashlight into my eyes and then asking me if I could name all the Teletubbies. I told her that Teletubbies were lame and then threw up on her shoes. Not to be evil, just because I had to, you know. She said I had a concussion and needed to stay in the hospital overnight so they could keep an eye on me.

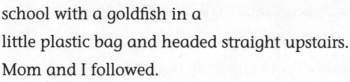

So, the day after Mark got the chemistry set he came home after school with a goldfish in a little plastic bag and headed straight upstairs. Mom and I followed.

"Did you go to a fair?" I asked.

"Moron." He shot me a look as he pulled his earphones out of his ears. "It's from the pet shop. For school. Science week."

"Why do you need . . . ?" Mom started to ask,

when Mark shoved a letter from his bag into her hand.

She read aloud: "Class 7M will be doing experiments on the effects of pollution on marine populations. Students will show photos of their experiments to the class tomorrow." She looked at Mark. "OK, if it's homework," she said as she headed down the stairs. "At least you're doing something green."

Mark put on his white scientist coat and took out his chemistry set. As he unpacked the box, I got that crawly-millipede feeling in my stomach again. Mark should have done one of those "Mwahaha!" **EVIL SCIENTIST** laughs at that point, but I guess he was still learning the ropes.

Mom shouted up from downstairs, "Mark, look after your brother while I run to the store. I'll be back soon." I heard the door close and looked over at Mark.

Normally, as soon as Mom left, Mark would start acting mostly evil to me. Like when he

caught me reading
his mint-condition
*Return of the Attack
of the Undead Zombie*
comic. He wrapped
me in beach towels
and wedged me in
the dog flap till the

neighbors complained about my shouting and
Mom had to come home from work to un-wedge
me. Oh, the good old *mostly* evil days. But now
that he was an actual **EVIL SCIENTIST**, he was too
busy to think of things to squeeze me into or trap
me under. There was definitely less torture, but
more shouting.

"Touch nothing, moron," Mark growled at me
as he went out to the hall closet.

He came back with the old goldfish bowl, filled
it in the bathroom sink, and dumped the fish
inside. I pressed my face up against the glass.
This goldfish was fatter than the ones from the

fair. It had big bulging eyes and a long wavy
tail with three fins. It kind of looked like a really
ugly bug-eyed mermaid, if you squinted enough.
Then, as I squinted at the fish, it squinted back.
Mark was too busy reading the back of a jar from
his chemistry set to notice. The fish swam up to
the side of the bowl and peered at me through
the glass, its little mouth opening and closing. I
know it sounds crazy, but I swear it looked like
the fish was saying, "Help me."

Mark unscrewed
the lid of the jar.
My millipede
feeling got
worse. He
took out some
test tubes and
mixed up a
bottle of a truly
evil-looking green
mixture.

"What are you doing?" I asked.

"Polluting," he grunted, and tipped some of the green stuff into the water with the fish.

"Stop! It could hurt the fish!" I shouted, and tried to grab the bottle.

Mark shoved me back on the carpet with one hand while he added some brown powder and gray flakes to the fishbowl. I tried to get up, but he held me firm by pushing his size-7 sneakers down on my chest. He grabbed his phone and snapped a picture of the fish swimming around in the gunky water.

"What will . . . it do to . . . the fish?" I gasped with the last bit of air left in my lungs.

"Dunno," he said. "That's the experiment." He laughed an absolutely perfect **EVIL SCIENTIST** laugh. Man, he was a fast learner. Then he put his phone back in his pocket. "I'll come back later to take another picture, and then I can flush it." Mark lifted his foot off my shirt and I sucked in a lungful of air.

"Flush what?" I spluttered.

"Duh, the fish." He put his earphones in again and headed back down the stairs, shouting back, "Remember, touch nothing, moron. Got it?"

"Got it," I said. But I totally didn't get it. I stood up and tried to rub off the footprint Mark had left on my T-shirt. Then I glanced over at the fishbowl. It didn't look good. The fish was squirming in the bowl and sucking in gulps of mucky water. Then it swam up to the glass again.

I stared through the cloudy green water, right

into the fish's big bulging eyes, and did the most dangerous thing I've ever done in my short life.

I touched it.

# CHAPTER 3

# FISH 911

I did more than touch it. I reached into the bowl and scooped it up with my fingers and ran to the bathroom.

"Come on, fish. Hang on. You'll be OK now," I muttered as I ran.

The fish was covered in the green gunk and it was flipping about in my hands. At least it was still moving, but it wouldn't last long, all gunked up like this. I tried to hold it in one hand while I turned on the tap and tried to wash it, but I could feel it wriggling through my fingers.

Then, *slurp!* It flipped out of my hand and landed in the toilet.

*Splash!*

I dropped down next to the bowl. The fish kind of bobbed around and swished its tail, but then it went still and leaned over. Our other goldfish all did that leaning thing too, just before they went belly up and died.

I raced to my bedroom and got my walkie-talkie. "Tom to Pradeep. Come in, Pradeep. Over," I said.

"Roger," Pradeep answered. "I mean Roger, Tom—or Tom, Roger. Anyway, I'm here. Over."

"Pradeep, it's a Code Red!" I shouted. "Over. Quick!"

We have this code of important stuff we both agreed on when we were back in first grade.

Yellow is stuff like: Girls are nearby.

Blue is stuff like: There's a dog digging up the gross food from our lunchboxes that we buried.

Orange is stuff like: There's a teacher/parent coming.

Red is the most important stuff you can imagine, like: Aliens are invading the neighborhood. Or escaped elephants are trampling the playground. Or somebody is murdering a goldfish.

If you're trying to figure out the system, it's not like traffic lights or anything. It's the color of jelly beans from least good to best.

"I'll be there on the double," Pradeep said and hung up.

I was still staring at the leaning fish in the toilet when Pradeep ran up the stairs. "In here," I called.

"What's up?" he asked.

I pointed to the fish.

Pradeep bent down and looked closely at it. "Did you go to a fair?" he asked.

"No, it's Mark's," I said. "Part of his **EVIL SCIENTIST** plan to murder a goldfish with green **EVIL SCIENTIST** stuff."

We leaned over the toilet bowl and stared at the fish again.

"Did you learn anything on your Cub Scout first-aid day that could help him?" I asked hopefully.

"We didn't do goldfish," he said.

The fish tilted to one side, then the other, then onto his back.

"Oh no, he's going belly up!" I shouted. I reached into the toilet and turned the fish right side up, but he just floated upside down again when I let go. "Pradeep, we need to do something! Quick! I told him he'd be OK. He's counting on me."

"It needs CPR," Pradeep said. "On a person you would press on their chest and count or you would shock them with those battery packs attached to paddles that they have in hospitals. I saw it on TV."

"We have batteries," I said. I ran into my room and took the battery out of my alarm clock. Then I raced back to see Pradeep laying the fish on the shelf by the sink. I put the openish end of the battery on him and *FLIP!* The fish jerked. I looked at Pradeep and I did it again. *FLIP, FLOP!* This time the fish started wriggling like it did when I first grabbed it out of the bowl. We quickly filled up the sink and dropped the fish in.

And it started swimming around!

"We did it!" I said. Pradeep and I did our secret celebration high five. Two slaps up, two

down, elbow bumps, knees, fist bumps, left,
right, left, right, then "We rock!" said at
the same time as we bumped fists in the
middle.

"You shocked him back to life," said Pradeep.
"Like Frankenstein in that movie. Hey, let's call
him Frankie—after the monster."

"Hello, Frankie," I said, tapping the side of the

sink. He stopped swimming and slowly turned around. And that's when I swear he looked me right in the eye and winked.

# CHAPTER 4

# FRANKENFISH

"Did you see that?" I turned to Pradeep.

"What?" Pradeep was drying his hands on the bathroom towel.

"The way Frankie looked at me? He winked!" I stared down at the goldfish, but now he was looking around in the normal way that goldfish do. You know, where one of their eyes is looking at the wall and the other eye is looking up your left nostril at the same time.

"Never mind," I said, shaking my head. "We've gotta get Frankie back in his bowl before Mark notices he's gone. Or else—"

"You're dead meat."
Pradeep finished my words.

We ran back into Mark's room to grab the bowl of gloopy green water.

"You can't put him back in the bowl. The gunge will kill him," Pradeep said.

"We can't put him in clean water. Mark will notice and kill *me*," I said. "And then he'll kill Frankie!"

We ran back to the bathroom, sat on the radiator and stared at Frankie swimming around in the sink.

Then I had an idea. "Hey, what if we make it green with safe stuff. Remember that green food coloring stuff your mom used last St. Patrick's Day? I mean, if it's OK for people to eat, it's gotta be OK for a fish to swim in, right?"

Pradeep thought for a sec. "It'll have to be."

Pradeep's mom isn't Irish, she just gets really

into holidays. You can pretty much name a holiday and Pradeep's mom has had a party for it. When we went over there for her St. Patrick's Day party, she had dyed everything green. We even had green finger sandwiches.

Which, it turns out, don't even have real fingers in them. Total false advertising. And she had green milkshakes and green cupcakes with green icing. It was cool except that when you eat seventeen green cupcakes in a row, it means you throw up in green.

"We have to get some of the green food coloring from your kitchen," I said.

"I can't go home," Pradeep said. "My mom

will make me stay for the Earth Day Polar Bear Pajama Party that she's having."

I looked at Pradeep with a face that said, I can't even ask why she would do that. He answered my face.

"She says the North Pole has really long nights and the polar bears sleep a lot, so they'd want a pajama party." He paused. "I told her it didn't work."

"Never mind. OK, I'll go and get the food coloring." I said. As I started for the stairs I could hear the *thump, thump, thump* of Mark's music coming through his headphones. He must be on the couch just by the steps. There was no way I could sneak past. "OK, I'm taking Escape Route 5." Pradeep and I had planned sixteen different escape routes from both our houses, just in case of a Code Red. Route 5 was out of my bathroom window. "Pradeep, it's up to you to stop Mark from coming upstairs before I get back."

"You can count on me," Pradeep said. "I'll think of something to keep him occupied."

He gave me a thumbs-up, then took a deep breath and headed downstairs to the TV room, where Mark was slumped over the couch.

"Can I say, that's a really cool white scientist

coat you're wearing," Pradeep said. I heard him start to tell Mark about the nature special on the National Geographic channel that shows you what's really in a crocodile's stomach.

Time for Escape Route 5. I opened the window of the bathroom and stood on the toilet lid to climb out onto the garage roof. Suddenly it looked a lot farther down to the roof than it did in the drawing we'd done in Pradeep's notebook. No going back now though. I edged out the window. Then I heard a *splash* and a *thwap*. Before I even turned around I knew what that sound was. It was the sound of a wet goldfish hitting a tiled floor.

# CHAPTER 5

# THAT'S NO ORDINARY GOLDFISH

"No, Frankie!" I said as I jumped off the toilet and scooped him up.

He wriggled in my hands as I dropped him back into the sink. He swam twice in a circle and then up to the surface, where he stared at me, his eyes glowing a bit green.

"You stay here. I'll be back." I climbed back onto the toilet seat and turned and pushed the window again, wide enough for me to crawl through. That was when I heard the next *splash* and then a *whoosh*!

Green and gold flashed past my right ear as Frankie leaped out of the window. I stuck my head out in time to see him land in a puddle of rainwater on the garage roof. Jumping down, I quickly dug the plastic bag he'd arrived in out of the trash. This was too weird. Frankie really wanted to go outside. None of the ping-pong-ball fish ever did anything like this.

Once I'd filled up the bag with water I scrambled out onto the roof.

"I guess you're coming with me then," I said as I scooped up Frankie from the puddle and plopped him in the bag. I tied a knot in the top and held the bag in my teeth as I climbed down the side of the garage. My feet felt for the top of the compost bin. Got it! From there I jumped down onto the lawn.

Escape Route 5 was a success (even carrying a fish). Result!

I ran around to the front of the house and peeked through the window. I could see Pradeep's back. He was sitting in a chair and Mark was standing in front of him showing him his chemistry set. If Pradeep could just keep Mark downstairs for a bit longer, then Frankie and I would be back before he noticed. In seconds I was at Pradeep's back door, inching it open.

His mom was inside making popcorn. Popcorn kernels popped and banged so loudly, she didn't hear the door open. She rolled some popcorn pieces in green marshmallow fluff and rolled some others in blue marshmallow fluff and then squished them into little round globes. Then she poured melted white chocolate over the top of each of the little earths. It took me a second, but then I got it. Melting polar ice caps. Cool.

"Samina," she called out, "can you come and help Mommy take out our party plates?"

Sami burst through the kitchen door dressed in mermaid pajamas with a blue-and-green tail swooshing behind her. The tail got caught in the

door, yanking her onto the floor with a *thud*. I covered my mouth so she couldn't hear me laugh.

And before you say anything, laughing at little sisters doing stupid things is totally not evil; it's not even mostly evil. It's just regular.

As Pradeep's mom went over to help her, Frankie and I moved over to the cupboard where all the party stuff was kept. I crouched low behind the counter and put Frankie on the floor in his bag so I could open the cupboard and reach inside.

"Samina, would you like to lick the chocolate bowl?" Pradeep's mom asked as she put Sami back on her feet and turned to take the chocolate-and-marshmallow popcorn balls out into the living room. I heard the kitchen door shut behind her.

Sami toddled over to the counter that we were hiding behind. "Bowl," she announced in that really serious way tiny kids have of saying stuff. She stuck her hands in the bowl, smeared them around and started to lick the chocolate. Then she squealed, "Fishy! Fishy!"

I peered around the corner to see Sami jumping up and down on the spot and Frankie

swishing his tail in circles and paddling his front fins at the same time to roll the bag toward her. How did he figure out how to do that?

"Fishy! Fishy!" Sami shouted again.

I jumped out from behind the counter. "Shhh, Sami!"

Her bottom lip started shaking in that earthquake warning—this tantrum is going to be a nine on the Richter scale—kind of way.

I scooped up Frankie off the floor in his bag and handed him to Sami. She gripped the top with her chocolatey fingers.

"I mean, shhh, quiet little fishy," I whispered.

"Shhh, little fishy." She giggled. She stared at Frankie in the bag. "Swishy little fishy," she said.

I ran back to the cupboard and searched. Flour, sugar, sprinkles, icing, tiny little icing polar bears . . . Aha! Food coloring. I grabbed the little green bottle and ran back to Sami and Frankie.

Sami was still holding the bag, but she was much quieter now. She just whispered "swishy little fishy" over and over. Frankie stared at her with his big green bulging eyes and she just stared ahead. What was with this goldfish? He could survive toxic gunge, jump out of windows, and now he could make the noisiest little kid on the planet go quiet. As I looked at Frankie a little lightbulb went on somewhere in the back of my head.

Frankie's glowing green eyes. They looked like the "Undead Gaze" that the zombies in Mark's comics used to hypnotize people. And Sami's stare! One of her eyes was looking at the wall and the other one was looking up my left nostril at the same time.

It was a goldfish stare!

Maybe I hadn't saved Frankie's life at all when I shocked him with the battery? Maybe I brought him back from the dead . . . and now Frankie was a Big Fat Zombie Goldfish! And somehow he had hypnotized my best friend's sister.

# CHAPTER 6

# DAWN OF THE ZOMBIE TODDLER

I had to get back to Pradeep. He'd know what
to do. Maybe they'd learned about hypnotized
little sisters in Cub Scouts? I grabbed Sami's slimy,
chocolatey hand and headed for the back door just
as Pradeep's mom came back into the kitchen.

"Oh, hello, Tom. I thought you and Pradeep
were playing at your house. Isn't Pradeep with
you?"

"Um, hi, Mrs. Kumar, um, Pradeep asked
me to come and get Sami 'cause my mom said
she could play with the new goldfish we got," I
mumbled. "Is that OK?"

"Swishy little fishy," Sami said again.

"Tell your mom that's fine, but Pradeep should bring Samina back in half an hour for dinner. Would you like to come as well? I can—"

"OK," I blurted out, pulling Sami by the hand. Pradeep's mom was still talking as we ran out the door and around the back of my house. I pushed Sami through the dog flap in the kitchen door (Escape Route 14) and then squeezed through myself.

Sami was still doing the freaky goldfish-stare thing and I knew I had to get Frankie back up the stairs and into his bowl with clean green water or Mark would completely kill me. I peeked around the corner into the living room, but Mark and Pradeep were gone. Then I heard Mark's mumbling voice upstairs.

Frankie started thrashing around in the water like mad at the sound of Mark's voice and I swear his eyes started glowing more than ever. I quickly pushed Sami and Frankie back into the kitchen.

"Just wait here," I said. "And remember, shhhh."

Sami put a chocolatey finger to her lips as she held the bag in the other arm like a baby doll. "Shhhh," she said.

OK, I know that it might seem strange to leave my friend's hypnotized little sister alone with the zombie fish that hypnotized her, but I don't know how to explain it, I just kind of knew she wouldn't be in danger with Frankie. I also knew, even back when my brother was mostly evil, Pradeep would totally be in danger with Mark. Zombie goldfish are like Code Blue in jelly bean terms, but **EVIL SCIENTIST** big brothers are definitely Code Red.

I snuck upstairs and slowly peered around the corner into Mark's room. Pradeep was on the floor. Oh no, I was too late! I could see his feet but not his body or his head, because Mark's desk was in the way. Pradeep wasn't moving at all. Mark must have knocked him out. He'd

gone completely evil
now. The millipedes
in my stomach
were having a
squirming party.

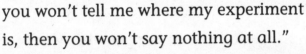

Mark stood in
front of Pradeep
and looked at the
goldfish bowl.
"Fine," he said. "If
you won't tell me where my experiment
is, then you won't say nothing at all."

Then I saw Pradeep's foot wiggle and heard
him trying to talk.

"Mmanything," he mumbled.

He sounded like he did the day we had the
green cupcake–eating contest at his mom's
and he was trying to say "No more cupcakes,
please" with a mouth completely squashed full
of cupcakes.

"Shut up," Mark said, and kicked Pradeep's

foot as he went out toward the bathroom. "I'm gonna put more water in the fishbowl. Stay put, moron."

I ran into my room so Mark wouldn't see me. When I heard him turn on the tap on the bathroom sink, I jumped up and tiptoed back to the doorway of Mark's room.

I had to get Pradeep's attention to check he was OK, so I made our secret "I need to get your attention to check you're OK" call, which is a cross between a snake hiss and a dolphin click.

Pradeep sat up as soon as he heard. He shuffled forward from behind the desk. His arms were stuck behind his back. Then I saw his face. His mouth was completely taped up with Scotch tape from ear to ear in one direction and right down his nose to his chin in the other. Just his nostrils were tape free. He even had little crossways bits of tape going across his cheeks and jaws. That's gotta hurt. I guess maybe telling Mark about what's in a crocodile's stomach wasn't such a great idea after all.

I gave him the thumbs-up sign and held up the little bottle of green coloring for him to see.

I think Pradeep smiled a little then. But it was pretty hard to tell for sure, with all the tape. Then Pradeep shook his head really hard.

That's when I felt the *thwack* to the back of my head and I saw the carpet in Mark's room come up to meet my face.

# CHAPTER 7

## A CLASSIC EVIL SCIENTIST TRAP

While my face was kissing the carpet, Mark pulled my arms back behind me and tied them together. Everything seemed a bit hazy after that, but he must have dragged me over to where Pradeep was sitting and put us back to back. He had piled up some comics and stuff next to us and there was a shadow of something over our heads. The next thing I knew, he was tying us together with the belt from his white coat. A classic **EVIL SCIENTIST** move.

Something dripped onto my face. It smelled disgusting. "Pradeep, what is that?" I asked as I wiped my chin on my shoulder.

"Mmark's mmot mma mmishmmowl mmilled mmoo ma mmop mmith mma mmoxic mmunky mmater mmalanced mmover mmour mmeads," Pradeep mumbled.

I looked up to see the goldfish bowl sitting on a wobbly tray balanced between two towers of comic books. Water was sloshing out of the bowl with every little move we made.

"Mark's got the fishbowl filled to the top with the toxic gunky water balanced over our heads?" I said, translating Pradeep's cupcake talk.

"How do you do that, moron?" Mark interrupted. "No, shut up. Don't tell me that. Tell me where the fish is!"

He leaned in so his face was right up against mine. I should have said something really cool like, "I guess they don't make EVIL SCIENTIST breath-freshener then?" But instead I just stared back at Mark, trying really hard to ignore the millipede feeling all over my body. Still, I didn't tell him where Frankie was.

"Fine." Mark stood up. "Morons, prepare to be gunged."

Then I heard a quiet voice say, "Swishy little fishy."

Sami was standing at the door of Mark's room with Frankie in the bag in her arms. His eyes were bright green and his tail was thrashing wildly. He was staring right at Mark.

Sami was looking mega–goldfish starey.

"Little moron?" Mark said. "Hey, she's staring up my nose and at the wall. It's freaking me out. Make her stop."

"It's the fish," I said. "He's hypnotized her and he can do it to you."

Pradeep mumbled, "Mma mmish mmas mmypmomized mmy mmister?"

"Yeah, sorry, I was going to tell you when— *thwack*. You know," I said.

Mark bent over to look more closely at the fish in the bag. Frankie's eyes glowed and Mark was starting to look a bit goldfish starey himself, when he suddenly took a pair of protective science-experiment goggles out of his **EVIL SCIENTIST** coat pocket and put them on. I had no idea **EVIL SCIENTISTS** had so many accessories.

"Like that's gonna work on me," he snorted. "Cool, the fish has come back with evil powers."

"He's not evil!" I shouted.

"Mma mmomminmmation mmof mmoxic mmemicals mmand mma mmattery mmock

46

mmust mmave mmiven mmim mmecial mmowers," Pradeep said.

"I guess the combination of toxic chemicals and the battery shock must have given him special powers, Pradeep, yes," I said.

"Can you stop doing that?!" Mark stomped his foot. "I already figured that out. I'm the **EVIL SCIENTIST** here, not your moron friend. Does he have a white coat? Nooooo. Is he even evil? Nooooo. So shut it!"

That was the most words Mark had ever said to me in his entire life.

Mark paced in front of us with his hands stuffed in the pockets of his coat for a minute. Then he stopped and looked at Frankie.

"OK, Fish, now you're *my* zombie goldfish. Just think of all the people we can hypnotize."

Frankie thrashed his tail and suddenly Sami lunged at Mark. She dropped the bag and tried to attack him. (As much as a three-year-old dressed in a mermaid suit flailing around can be called an attack.) "Swishy little fishy!" she squealed.

Mark just picked Sami up and wedged her, bottom first, into his *Star Wars* waste-paper basket. Her mermaid tail flapped helplessly against Chewbacca's face as she struggled to get free. But instead of screaming the house down, she just stared the fishy stare. Wow, Sami was really zombied out.

"You need better minions, Fish," Mark said as he picked up the bag from the floor. "Now, let's see if we can make the whole school into fish zombies."

"You won't get away with it, Mark," I said, pulling at the white belt tying Pradeep and me together. "You may be an **EVIL SCIENTIST**, but you're still only twelve. Mom will be home soon and she won't let you hypnotize the school, or toxic-gunge us, or take Frankie anywhere."

Just at that moment Mark's phone rang. "Hi, Mom. No, Tom's fine. He's playing with

his moron friend and his moron sister." Mark stopped to listen.

"OK, his little friend and his little sister. No, you stay and have coffee with your friend." Then he paused again. "Oh, sorry, no, Tom can't come to the phone right now—he and Pradeep are kinda tied up."

Mark covered the phone with his hand. "Mwahahaha," he laughed. Mark was getting way too comfortable with this new evil-laugh thing.

Then he spoke again. "I'm fine. I'm just finishing my science homework."

# CHAPTER 8

# THE GREAT ESCAPE

He hung up the phone and went to put it in his pocket. As he did, Frankie twisted and shook free from Mark's grasp. The bag landed on the carpet and Frankie started to roll for the door. Yes! Frankie was escaping.

Mark walked over to Pradeep and me and tapped the goldfish bowl above our heads. "Fish!" he called. "Say good-bye to the morons."

Frankie paused and looked back at us.

"Go, Frankie!" I shouted. "Get away now!"

I felt Pradeep's body go all tense as he prepared for the gunge to hit us, but the glow in Frankie's eyes faded as he looked at me.

I shook my head and mouthed the words, "Frankie, go!" But Frankie stopped thrashing in his bag and stayed still.

"Good choice, Fish." Mark walked over and scooped up the bag. "Remember, if you won't help me, then it's flush time for you."

"Noooo!" I shouted.

"Mmnooo!" Pradeep moaned.

"Fishy!" Sami squealed and held out her hands.

"Now, let's get ready to hypnotize Mom when she gets back," Mark said as he strode out of the room clenching Frankie's bag tight in his fist.

OF COURSE I WILL LET YOU WATCH TV WHENEVER YOU WANT AND MAKE SURE YOUR EVIL SCIENTIST COAT IS BRILLIANT WHITE FOR WHEN YOU TAKE OVER THE WORLD. ANYTHING ELSE, DEAR?

Mark slammed the door. We looked up to see the bowl balanced above our heads rocking back and forth. It was going to fall!

I felt Pradeep trying to reach up to grab the knot in the belt around us, but his wrists were tied too tight. The bowl wobbled more with every move we made. Green slimy water dripped on the back of my neck. Pradeep stretched his fingers as far as he could but it wasn't enough. I squashed closer to him to try to give the belt some slack so he could reach.

"Mmearly mmot mmit!" he said as his fingers pulled on the knot behind his back. "Mmyes!" He loosened the knot and I felt the belt drop away.

"Roll!" I shouted as we both rolled in opposite directions just as the goldfish bowl slammed on to the carpet between us, spilling toxic water across the floor.

I ran over to Pradeep and pulled the tape off his mouth, leaving sticky pink stripes across his face.

"Thanks, Pradeep. How did you do that?"
I asked as I pulled the last loop of belt off my
wrists.

"We did knots at Cubs last week. That was a
quarterman's noose—not too tricky to undo if
you know how," he answered.

Then we went to help Sami out of the trash
can. She hugged Pradeep around the neck as I
eased Chewbacca off her bottom.

"Now to get Frankie," I said.

That's when we heard it—a sound that I never
found terrifying until that day. We heard a fatal
flush.

# CHAPTER 9
# THE FATAL FLUSH

We all ran to the bathroom door to listen.

"You see, Fish," we heard Mark say, "that's where you're going unless you help me."

Then we heard water splashing.

"That must be Frankie sploshing around in his bag," I said. "He hasn't flushed him yet."

"Swishy little fishy," Sami chanted. She was still all zombie-fish eyes.

"We have to get Mark out of there," Pradeep whispered.

"His phone," I said. "He'll answer his phone. You take Sami back home and call him from your house. Tell him you're gonna tell your mom and he'll come over to try and stop you."

"What will you do?" Pradeep asked.

"I'll run in and grab the bag with Frankie in it while Mark's gone."

Pradeep took Sami downstairs. I heard the dog flap slap shut and waited behind the bedroom door so Mark wouldn't see me when he came out. It seemed like hours of millipedes doing laps in my stomach before I heard Mark's phone ring.

"Mwahahaha—mwahahaha." He had changed his ringtone to his evil laugh! That was hardcore **EVIL SCIENTIST** stuff.

Then I heard him speak. "Yeah? Moron? No, you talk, you die." He stormed out of the bathroom and slammed the door behind him. I stayed where I was. I heard him go into his bedroom and kick the goldfish bowl on the floor. "Stupid morons' stupid trap," he grunted. He trudged down the stairs and I heard the front door slam shut behind him.

Yes! It was working.

Rescue Frankie Plan—Part One: Mark on his way to Pradeep's to stop him from telling his mom Mark's **EVIL SCIENTIST** plans. Check!

I just had to hope that Mark wouldn't actually kill Pradeep if his mom was there. I crossed my fingers and even my toes inside my sneakers.

Rescue Frankie Plan—Part Two: Actually rescue the fish. Nearly check.

I had my hand on the doorknob of the

bathroom door when I heard that horrible sound again.

I heard the toilet flush. . . .

I ran into the bathroom and saw the water spiraling down the toilet bowl.

"Frankie, no!" I shouted, but he was already gone.

# CHAPTER 10
# MISSION UNFLUSHABLE

Then I heard a *splash* outside. I looked up and saw the open bathroom window. I climbed up on the toilet and looked out. There was Frankie, rolling his plastic bag out of the puddle on the garage roof. Then he rolled himself along the gutter, dropped down onto the rain barrel and, with a final dismount, *flumped* onto the grass.

I punched the air. He was safe. But I was dead meat when Mark found out the fish was gone.

Maybe I could convince Mark that I'd flushed Frankie? No, he'd never buy it. And he'd kill me anyway, just because he could. I'd be better off escaping with Frankie.

I was just about to climb out the window and follow him when I heard the next noise. It sounded like someone falling down the back steps, bouncing off the little trampoline, and crashing into a sandbox. That couldn't be Frankie making that noise. But if it wasn't Frankie, then who was it?

I ran downstairs and out the door. Mark was lying facedown in the sandbox, groaning. The little trampoline had been put at the bottom of the steps, which were smeared with white chocolate.

My first thought was: I'm really good at guessing stuff just from sounds.

My second thought was: White chocolate? It's gotta be Sami.

"Again! Again!"

I heard the giggling voice from behind me.

Sami was carrying a bowl of chocolate and licking her fingers. She started bouncing on the trampoline. "You were funny," she said

to Mark. "Again! Please? Again!"

Mark just groaned.

Pradeep came running across the garden toward us. He stopped when he saw Sami. "Sami, you're supposed to be inside with Mom." Then he looked at the steps and back at her hands. "Sami, did you . . . ?"

"Frankie must have hypnotized her to do it," I said.

Sami smiled. Her hands were still covered in chocolate but her expression was normal. She didn't look hypnotized anymore.

I waved my hand in front of her face to check.

"Hi, Tom," she said, and waved back at me.

She definitely didn't have the goldfish stare anymore. But she also didn't have the goldfish.

"Where's fishy?" I asked her in an "I'm trying not to panic but really starting to panic" kind of way.

"Swishy little fishy," she said, still bouncing. "Fishy rolled away."

We looked around for Frankie. Under the trampoline, around the bike shed, under the shrubs. No good.

Mark's groans started to become words. Things like "Stupid morons," and, "They'll be sorry," and, "I can smell chocolate." He was starting to move too.

Then Sami squealed again, "Swishy little fishy!" and pointed to the top of the jungle-gym slide.

There was Frankie. He was rolling his plastic bag onto Mark's skateboard. The skateboard was pointed down the slide, straight at the sandbox and straight at Mark's head.

# CHAPTER 11

## REVENGE OF THE ZOMBIE GOLDFISH

Frankie's eyes were bright glow-in-the-dark green and his tail was swishing hard back and forth in the water.

The goldfish was set on revenge. I looked at Mark lying at the bottom of the slide. My fists clenched at the thought of him trying to hurt Frankie, but could I really stand by and let Frankie hurt him?

"Um, your goldfish is trying to kill your brother!" Pradeep shouted.

"Not if I can help it," I said. And then I did the second most dangerous thing I've ever done in my life. I tried to stop Frankie.

Frankie swished his tail hard, and the skateboard started to roll down the slide, picking up speed as it went.

"Fishy! Wheeeeeee!" Sami yelled.

I raced to the bottom of the slide and threw myself between Mark and the skateboard.

I could see Frankie's eyes as he rode the skateboard down toward me. They changed to a soft green and he swished his tail back and forth wildly. He wanted me to get out of the way.

I shook my head and held my ground. I closed my eyes, waiting for the skateboard to hit me. Concussion number two, here I come. Then I heard the skateboard jump off the side of the slide. I looked up to see it flip midair, like when the boarders at the park do half-pipes and twists.

Except this was a goldfish in a plastic bag, not a skateboarding kid. And the thing about goldfish in bags is that when the board goes upside down they have no way to hang on. The skateboard flew over me and Mark and then Frankie started to fall. He must have been ten feet in the air.

I rolled over onto my back and held out my hands to catch him. The bag hit my hands but I couldn't hold it. It *splatted* on my chest and the bag burst open. Water sprayed everywhere and Frankie was left flip-flopping around on my T-shirt.

"No!" I shouted. "Frankie!" I jumped up, cupping him in my hands. "I've got you, Frankie," I said as I turned to Pradeep. "Get some water! Quick!"

Frankie's goldfish mouth was opening and closing as if he were gasping for breath. His eyes were still the soft green color. He flicked his tail and wriggled, and then he stopped moving completely. "Hang on, Frankie!" I screamed.

Pradeep ran over to the slide with a watering can full of rainwater that he had grabbed from next to the shed. I dropped Frankie into it.

Pradeep, Sami, and me all sat around the watering can and stared at Frankie, unmoving in the water. "You turned the skateboard on purpose, didn't you? You didn't want to hurt me," I said.

Mark was still lying in the sandbox, moaning,

"The goldfish? My skateboard? Why am I wet?"

Frankie floated belly up in the watering can. He didn't move a fin.

"Swishy little fishy?" Sami said, sniffling. Her bottom lip started to wobble again. Not in a Richter-scale-level tantrum kind of way but in a sadder than a little kid ought ever to feel kind of way.

"He's gone," I said. The millipedes that were swimming in my stomach curled up into a big heavy millipede lump.

"I'm sorry," said Pradeep.

"Not swishy?" whispered Sami. A tear rolled down her cheek and dripped off her snotty nose into the watering can.

And that's when it happened. Frankie started to swish his tail. Just a little at first, then his gills started flapping and his mouth opened and closed and then he flipped over and started swimming in circles around and around.

"Fishy!" said Sami, and hugged the watering can.

"Frankie, you're back!" I said, hardly able to believe that he was swimming around again.

"Who's a good zombie fish?" I said, and stroked him gently behind the gills.

"Hey, you know what we just discovered?" Pradeep said.

"I know!" I said. "That the one thing more powerful than a battery for bringing a fish back to life is . . ."

Pradeep said with me at the same time, "Toddler snot."

# CHAPTER 12

## THE RETURN OF THE MOMMY

*Beep, beep.*

We heard Mom's car pull into the drive.

"Oh no!" I said.

Pradeep and I quickly ran over to Mark and helped him sit up. He was still holding on to his head where he had banged it when he fell into the sandbox.

Sami just sat there, still hugging the watering can.

Mom came straight around the back of the house and ran over to us. She could tell there was something wrong. Moms have this thing where they know stuff that should be impossible to know. Like that you didn't eat your carrot sticks at lunch, or that it was you who put the ham slice in the CD player to see what ham sounded like, or that your undead zombie goldfish hypnotized your neighbor's daughter and then tried to kill your **EVIL SCIENTIST** big brother but at the last minute changed its mind to save your life. You know, that kind of thing.

I took one look at Mom and was sure she would figure it out. It was so obvious what had happened.

But the first thing she said was, "What on earth happened here?"

"We were just playing," Pradeep said right away. "Um, the game got a little messy, um . . . and wet and um . . ."

He was talking really fast and looking really guilty. Mom was definitely going to get that something was up.

"Fishy is swishy!" Sami shouted. "Yaaaay!"

"Oh, that's sweet. You let Samina play with your fish, Mark," Mom said. "But why do you have the fish outside in a watering can?"

"It needed some fresh air," I said, which Mom is always telling us that we need, so it must be true for fish, too.

Although usually when Mom tells us to go outside, it's because she wants to talk to Dad alone, or shout at Aunt Sarah on the phone.

"OK," Mom's voice said in a normal kind of way, but her face was really saying, *What are they up to?*

"Mark, are you all right?" she added.

Mark rubbed his head. He looked over at me and Pradeep, and then at Sami and the watering can.

"The goldfish tried to kill me," he said. "I tripped and fell in the sandbox and then it aimed the skateboard at me."

Mom went over to Mark and felt his head for bumps. She's an expert bump finder after all these years. I bet she could be a doctor in bumps and stuff.

"You banged your head pretty bad, Mark." She held her fingers in front of Mark and said, "How many am I holding up?"

"It tried to kill me," Mark mumbled.

Mom looked over at me and Pradeep. "What happened?"

Then I heard myself say the most untrue thing ever: "Mark was being really nice, playing with Sami in the sandbox and on the trampoline."

"Bouncy, bouncy, crash!" said Sami, now jumping on the trampoline with the watering can.

I leaned over and gently took the can from her.

"Then he did a trick bounce that made Sami laugh," Pradeep said, which isn't really a lie, because he did do that even though he didn't mean to do it.

"He must have hit his head when he fell," I said.

"Oh, poor you," Mom said to Mark as she rubbed his head. "But what's this about the goldfish?"

She helped him stand up, and he walked over to where I was standing with the watering can. He stared at Frankie. The goldfish started thrashing around in the water like mad again and his eyes went bright green.

"Mom, look at the goldfish," Mark said, pointing wildly at the watering can. "It's gone nuts. It really tried to kill me!"

Pradeep and I shot each other a look. We couldn't say anything out loud, but our faces said that we needed a new color jelly bean code, because this was way beyond a Code Red.

Mom *couldn't* look now. She'd see Frankie being all zombie fish. Then she would let Mark flush him for sure, or she'd send him off to some

government place
where they
keep pets that
have gone all
supernatural
and
dangerous.

"All right,"
she said.
"I'll look at
the goldfish." She
marched over toward us.

We were doomed.

# CHAPTER 13

# GOT MY ZOMBIE EYE ON YOU

"Please, Frankie," I whispered, as I peered into the watering can. "Mark's not completely evil, really. I won't let him hurt you, but you can't try and kill him again. OK?"

Frankie stopped thrashing and looked up out of the watering can at me. His eyes stopped glowing and he got that goldfish stare back again.

Mom leaned over the watering can. "Is that fish staring up my nostril?" she said.

Pradeep and I looked into the can. "Phew . . . I mean, yes, I guess," I said.

"You said the goldfish was trying to kill you,

Mark?" Mom said, going back to him and feeling his head for bumps again. "Was that before or after you bumped your head?"

"Definitely after," Pradeep said.

"Yeah, he started talking weird just after he fell," I said.

"Bouncy, bouncy, bang," Sami said, nodding her head.

"The kid was in on it. She was all goldfish starey and she was out to get me too," Mark said, backing away from Sami.

Sami giggled. "Swishy little fishy."

"Argh!" Mark yelled, and ran and hid behind Mom.

"OK, we need to go to the hospital to get them to look at your head. I think you've got a concussion." She led Mark over to the edge of the sandbox to sit him down. "I'm going to go speak to your mom, Pradeep. I'm sure she won't mind looking after you all until Mark and I get back from the hospital." She took Sami's hand.

"You come with me, Samina, to see Mommy."
She turned to me and Pradeep. "I'll be back in
a second. You boys please look after him, OK?
Keep him talking."

Pradeep and I looked at each other nervously.
It was like we were being left with a tiger that
was just waking up and we knew he was going to
wake up pretty mad.

ROCK-A-BYE, BABY . . .

"How you feeling, Mark?" I said quietly.

Mark growled in that **EVIL SCIENTIST** big-brother way. Then he jumped up and leaned over Pradeep and me.

"You morons and the stupid goldfish won't win," he said. "But it doesn't matter, because as soon as I get home that fish is flushed and I'll stick your moron heads down the—"

But he didn't get to finish his threat. Frankie leaped out of the watering can, his eyes glowing a shining green. He started flapping his tail back and forth, whacking Mark across the face.

"Ow, ow, get it off! Get it off!" Mark said, and fell backward into the sandbox.

I scooped up Frankie in my hands and plopped him back into the watering can.

"I don't think you'll be flushing anything, Mark," I heard myself saying in a really strong voice, like I was on some TV cop show or something. "I think you are gonna leave me and Pradeep and Sami and Frankie alone," I said.

"Who's Frankie?" Mark said.

"My goldfish," I said, looking down at Frankie swimming around in the can. "And I wouldn't mess with him, because he can kick your butt."

Pradeep stepped forward. "Um, yeah, right. Like Tom said," he mumbled, and smiled at me.

# CHAPTER 14
# ZOMBIE SLEEPOVER

Mom raced back over from Pradeep's house. "OK, boys, thanks for looking after Mark." She winked at me and ruffled my hair. "You can act very grown-up sometimes, can't you? When you put your mind to it."

Frankie splashed in his watering can.

"I think we should get Frankie back into his bowl for the night," I said. "He's had enough air."

"Pradeep's mom said you can have your dinner there and then sleep over. It might be best. You never know how long the hospital will take. Remember when you had a concussion from running into that door? Why is it always my boys?" She shook her head. "Come on, Mark."

She helped him up from the sandbox and took him to the car. He was still talking about the fish being out to get him. Mom just nodded.

"Oh, and Mark," I yelled to him as Mom was pulling out of the drive, "don't worry about the pictures for your experiment. We'll take some good ones for you."

The last thing I saw as Mom rounded the corner toward the hospital was Mark banging on the back window mouthing the words, "Moron . . . No!"

Pradeep and I went in and got Frankie's goldfish bowl from upstairs, washed it out, and then headed over to Pradeep's house for the night. We decided that Frankie deserved a sleepover too. And Sami wanted to play with him again. After dinner, we got into our pajamas and had the marshmallow-popcorn earths with the white chocolate melting ice caps. And we took lots of cool pictures of Frankie.

Mom phoned Pradeep's house to say that she was staying with Mark because the doctors wanted to keep him overnight so they could keep an eye on him. I told Mom to make sure it wasn't a very big eye if they could help it. He is my big brother after all. And I think from now on he'll probably go back to just being mostly evil. As long as Frankie's around—my big fat zombie goldfish friend (and bodyguard).

When Pradeep's mom put Sami to bed, Pradeep and I got out our sleeping bags and told each other scary zombie stories. Telling scary stories is one of the top things about sleepovers. But THE top thing about sleepovers now is if we scare ourselves too much, we've always got a zombie goldfish nightlight to make everything seem brighter, and a bit green. How cool is that?

# RULES THE SCHOOL!

# CHAPTER 1

# THE EVIL COMPUTER GENIUS

You know how your voice sounds different when you're doing different stuff? Like, you have a "running" voice or a "jumping" voice or a "stuck in a pretzel shape because you tried to fit into a tiny box" voice? Well, I heard Pradeep shouting outside this morning and he definitely had an "upside down" voice.

"I'm a moron and you're a genius," he mumbled.

I looked out of the kitchen window as I filled up Frankie's plastic bag in the sink, and there was Pradeep, hanging upside down off the jungle gym.

"Louder, moron!" Sanj ordered, sitting on top of Pradeep's feet and dangling him off the metal railing. "And can you *please* articulate?"

"I am a moron and you are a genius!" Pradeep shouted, without mumbling this time.

"Come on, Frankie, it's a Code Red situation! Pradeep's in trouble!" I said, scooping Frankie out of the sink and into his bag. We ran into the yard.

"Good," Sanj said, letting go of Pradeep's feet. Pradeep slid through the monkey bars and splatted onto the grass.

"Ah look, your little moron friend has come to help," Sanj said as he jumped down from the jungle gym. "And he's brought his pet fish with him. How sad is that? The ugly little moron kid has an ugly little moron pet." He smiled a creepy evil smile at Frankie.

Frankie desperately head-butted the side of the bag, trying to get out. His eyes lost their normal goldfish stare and instead glowed a bright, angry green. He was in full zombie attack mode.

"Pathetic morons," Sanj said to himself as he strode off down the road.

I went over to Pradeep. "Are you OK?"

Pradeep was rubbing his head. "Yeah."

Frankie thrashed in his bag and glared down the road after Sanj.

"Wow, he normally just does that when he sees

Mark," I said. "He's still holding a grudge over the whole 'Mark trying to murder him with toxic gunge and flush him down the toilet' thing, but I think Frankie has just added Sanj to his hit list too."

Pradeep bent down to talk to Frankie. "Look, I'm OK. Nothing broken." He turned to me. "At least I'm taller now, so when Sanj drops me, I don't have so far to fall."

"True." I nodded.

It had been about six months since Pradeep's brother, Sanj, last dropped Pradeep off the jungle gym. He'd been away at some boarding school for "the gifted," which just sounded like a great place to go to school.

Sanj had always been a genius, but yesterday he became an actual Evil Computer Genius when he got kicked out of the gifted school. He hacked into its super-encrypted un-hackable computer system and changed all the other kids' grades to zero and his grade to one gazillion.

Now, I know what you're thinking. A real-life actual Evil Computer Genius living next door to a real-life actual Evil Scientist like my big brother, Mark. What are the odds? Well, Pradeep figured it out yesterday afternoon. It is seven million, three hundred and forty-four thousand, six hundred and twenty-three to one. Which is about the same odds as winning five lotteries all at once and having the prize money delivered to you by a team of bicycle-riding chimpanzees. At least that's what Pradeep told me. He found the answer on the Internet.

Anyway, Pradeep's brother, Sanj, has a real IQ certificate to prove he's an actual genius. He used to make us look at the piece of paper a lot when he first got it. And, just to make sure we really *saw* it, he used to press our faces against it on the floor while he sat on us. He didn't need a certificate to prove he was mostly evil. We knew that already.

I grabbed my backpack and carefully packed Frankie inside, placing his bag in the bottom of a Tupperware box.

"You're bringing Frankie to school?" Pradeep asked.

"I can't leave him at home after he got all green-eyed and thrashy with Sanj. He might break out and zombie someone! What if Mom saw him like that? Or Mark came home early?"

You see, the last time they were at home alone together, Mark tried to deep-freeze Frankie. Luckily, I found him pretty quickly when I used the ice dispenser on the fridge door and got a zombie fish cube. You know, I don't actually think Frankie minded the freezer that much. He just didn't like being next to the fish fingers.

"Trust me, Pradeep," I said as we headed off down the road toward the school, "Frankie is safer with us today."

# CHAPTER 2

# THE CREATURE FROM THE GREEN LAGOON

Pradeep and I got to school just before the breakfast counter closed. That's when I realized the difference between school breakfast and a big fat zombie goldfish. One is a scary green bulging lump, swimming in a pool of toxic gunge, and the other is a fish.

I stared down at my plate as I went through the cafeteria line, and my green lump jiggled as I moved.

The lunch lady tapped the protective lunch-lady glass with her fingernail. "More egg?" she asked. I shook my head and pushed through the line.

"It's an egg!" I said to Pradeep as I got to the cereal section of the counter.

"Ahhh," he said.

Pradeep was getting his usual. He's eaten the same breakfast every day since he discovered it in first grade. Choc Rice Pops on toast. If there is ever a Choc Rice Pops shortage, then Pradeep's breakfast world will end.

"Should we get something for Frankie to eat?" Pradeep asked.

Ever since we've had Frankie, we've been trying to figure out what zombie goldfish eat. At first we were scared that it might be brains. I mean, that's what all the comic books and movies tell you, right? But the problem is:

a) Zombie goldfish only have a couple of rotten teeth;

b) Brains float;

c) Goldfish have no hands;

d) Even if they could hold the brain still . . . zombie goldfish only have a couple of rotten teeth.

Therefore . . .

e) Brains would make a zombie goldfish really mad.

What we eventually realized is that zombie goldfish like to eat anything green, like green breadcrumbs (the moldier the better), or green bits of algae scraped up from the side of the pond.

"I don't think Frankie's hungry," I answered. "He had some green cupcake crumbs before school."

My backpack started to wobble from side to side on my back. Frankie must have been thrashing around. I unzipped my bag to check on him.

"I'm still not sure it's a good idea to have Frankie in school," Pradeep said.

"We had to bring him to school, Pradeep," I said. "If we left him alone with Mark, it might be Mark who ended up in the freezer."

"Hey, morons!"

I heard a chilling voice behind me, and Frankie swished his tail so hard that he made his plastic bag tip out of the Tupperware box. I turned him the right way up and re-zipped my backpack.

"Same stupid school, same stupid morons. Mwhahahaha." Mark laughed his Evil Scientist laugh. No, it couldn't be. Not him? Not here? Not now?

"No way," I said as I turned around.

"Way, moron," said Mark, flicking up the collar of his Evil Scientist white coat. "I'm at your school today. I gotta do an important experiment in the science lab."

"Why *our* science lab?" Pradeep asked.

"The lab in my school kinda blew up," Mark said. Cue evil laugh again. "So I've been sent to this dump for the day."

This wasn't good. Frankie was in school. Mark was in school. I had to think what to do, and fast.

# CHAPTER 3

# THE TRULY EVIL PLAN

In my head I scrolled through the list of "Frankie Evacuation Plans" that Pradeep and I had worked out on the walk to school.

There was just one that didn't seem to require a jet-pack. The only choice was for me to pretend to throw up and get sent home from school, taking Frankie with me.

The only problem was that the teachers were pretty good at spotting real vs. fake vomit. Kids tried to use applesauce mixed with ketchup, peanut butter and orange juice, or the classic baby-food trick, but teachers knew they were faking and just sent the kids back to class, still covered in applesauce and ketchup. No, I had to *really* get sick. But how?

The answer was staring me in the face. The green slimy breakfast egg was looking up at me from my plate, like a big wobbly Cyclops. All I had to do was eat the egg.

I grabbed Pradeep's Choc Rice Pops spoon from his hand and scooped up the egg. I gave Pradeep a look that said, "I am making the ultimate sacrifice for friend and fish."

He nodded respectfully, knowing what I was about to do.

I lifted the spoon and closed my eyes.

"Gulp!" Mark slurped down the egg from my spoon.

"Too slow, moron!" he said, then burped a perfect smelly Evil Scientist burp and headed out of the cafeteria doors.

The burp was nearly gross enough to make me sick, but not quite.

*Bbbrrrrrrriiiiiiiiiiiiiiiiiinnnnnnnnngggggggggggggg!* The fire alarm blared.

Everyone ran out into the hallway.

"There's no way Mark could have blown up our science lab already, right?" I said to Pradeep.

The teachers were assembling people in

lines at the classroom doors, ready to exit the building. But the alarm stopped. Then the TVs that were in the hallway by the front desk (you know, the ones that usually show pictures of the swimming team coming twenty-seventh in a race, or advertise a sale at the uniform shop) all came on at the same time. The secretary's computer screen switched on too. And the whiteboard screens in the classrooms all showed the same letters scrolling across them: B B E D L A M.

Suddenly a voice boomed out of all the speakers. It had one of those distort-effect things on it, so the person talking sounded kind of like a robot.

"Now we got your atten—" one person started to say, but then there was a shuffling sound and a different, snootier robot voice said, "No, let me . . . Ahem. Now that we have your attention. We want you to know that this school will soon be run by BBEDLAM. We've taken over."

"I'm sure bedlam only has one *b*," Pradeep said.

"And we know that there is usually only one *b* in bedlam. We're not morons, we are being original, OK, so get over it. Where was I? . . . Oh yes, BBEDLAM has taken over the school. You may now go about your pathetically ordinary lives and await further instruction. There is nothing that can stop us."

"Except the moron fish," the other voice butted in. My backpack swung from side to side as Frankie thrashed around.

"Be quiet!" shouted the snooty voice. Then there was what sounded like someone being elbowed in the ribs. "We are live on air, remember!" The snooty robot cleared his throat and continued, "Nothing can stop us now, so don't even try."

Just before all the TVs, computers, and whiteboards switched off I thought I heard the first voice say, "Aww, you cut it off before my evil laugh."

Pradeep shot me a look that said, "They said *fish*, right?" but I didn't really understand the look so he said out loud, "They said *fish*, right?"

I nodded and shot him back a look that said, "And they said *moron*. And they talked about an evil laugh." Pradeep didn't really get that look either so I said it again, out loud. Then I said we had to practice our secret looks because we were both kind of rusty.

We agreed that the first weird robot voice must have been Mark. Frankie reacted to the voice as soon as he heard it. Pradeep was sure the other one was Sanj. But what was Sanj doing here and why was he with Mark? They aren't even friends. The only thing they have in common is being mostly evil to me and Pradeep.

This wasn't good. You know that crawly millipede feeling that I got in my stomach when Frankie was first gunged by Mark? Well, I got

it again, only this time the

millipedes invited over a couple of cockroaches

and a tarantula for good measure.

# CHAPTER 4
# THE RISE OF BBEDLAM

We were all sitting in the hall for assembly, listening to Mrs. Prentice, the principal, lecture us about the misuse of school computers and illegal tampering with the fire alarm. Then she said, "I'll find out who did this and it would be easier for the purple-traitors if they just came forward now."

Mrs. Prentice looked at me and Pradeep a lot while she was talking. For about two seconds I thought about telling her that Pradeep's Evil Computer Genius big brother and my Evil Scientist big brother were somehow behind all this. But then I thought that's probably exactly

what a purple-traitor would say. Even though I wasn't really sure what a purple-traitor* was, I was definitely sure that I didn't want to be one. I don't even like purple, especially in jelly beans.

Pradeep and I knew we had to find out what was going on, and find out now. We each got bathroom passes from our teachers but left the hall by separate doors, so that Mrs. Prentice couldn't follow both of us. She must have thought I looked more suspicious, because she followed me, which gave Pradeep the opportunity to get away. I managed to lose her in the art room by hiding behind Darren Schultz's easel. Then I doubled back to catch up with Pradeep.

Pradeep snuck up to the computer lab ahead of me and peered around the door. It's where we had our first class anyway, but we needed to get in there before the other kids came out of assembly. I listened carefully for Pradeep's top secret "The coast is clear" call. Which, it turns out, was "Tom, there's no one here!"

* Pradeep looked up "purple-traitor" later online and told me that the word is actually "perpetrator," which apparently has nothing to do with being purple or being a traitor. How boring is that?

Not his best.

I went into the classroom and carefully placed my backpack on the floor.

"OK, we need to find out everything we can about BBEDLAM," I said, thinking that I sounded like the guy in spy movies who tells the spies what to do at the beginning of the movie but then never actually gets to do any of the cool adventure stuff himself. I decided I didn't want to be that guy so I said, "You know how to do that, right, Pradeep?"

He was way ahead of me. Pradeep was already sitting at one of the computers, typing away.

"I think I've found BBEDLAM's website," he said. "If Mark and Sanj are working together, then maybe they're out to get us with this BBEDLAM thing? Why else would they want to take over our school?"

"You're paranoid, Pradeep. They probably just want to take over the school to make the cafeteria only serve mega choc chunk ice cream

or make all the teachers dress as comic-book characters every day or something."

"That's just what you would do if you took over the school, right?" Pradeep asked.

"Maybe," I answered. "But I still don't think Mark and Sanj's evil plans have anything to do with us. Anyway, most evil geniuses just want power for the sake of it, don't they? And they never do anything really cool with it, like cover the earth in a giant bubblegum bubble or make everyone speak backwards or anything, which would be kind of—"

I was cut off by a loud Evil Scientist laugh that sounded from the speaker on the computer. "Mwhaaahaahaahaa!" Then little animated icons popped up on the screen.

"Hey, that little one looks like you, Pradeep," I said. "It's even got glasses and a Cub Scout kerchief."

"And there's you," Pradeep said, pointing to a little icon rolled in a rug and wedged in a tiny dog flap in a tiny door.

The Evil Scientist laugh got louder and then a giant sneaker appeared at the top of the screen and stomped the little Tom and Pradeep flat.

It was like seeing my worst nightmare turned into a video game.

"Or I could be wrong about the whole it's-not-about-us thing," I said.

The word BBEDLAM splatted across the computer screen and then a word appeared by each letter to spell out:

# BIG
# BROTHERS'
# EVIL
# DEEDS
# TO [PLEASE IGNORE ADDITIONAL "TO"]
# LITTLE
# ANNOYING
# MORONS

**BBEDLAM's Corporate Statement: BBEDLAM is a top-secret organization founded on the premise of doing high-quality evil deeds to little moron brothers and achieving world domination.**

Wow, Sanj was right. BBEDLAM was out to get us, and little brothers everywhere. We had to stop them.

"Pradeep, can you block the website or wipe it or something?" I asked.

"I don't know. Sanj is the Evil Computer Genius, not me," Pradeep said.

Then, while we were looking at the screen,
more words started to appear:

**LITTLE ANNOYING MORON KIDS WILL BE
TURNED INTO OUR SUB-ORNAMENTS**

Then those words were quickly deleted and
this was typed instead:

# LITTLE ANNOYING MORON SIBLINGS WILL BE TURNED INTO SUBORDINATES AND USED TO HELP ACHIEVE WORLD DOMINATION [EVENTUALLY]

"Hey! They're updating the site right now!" Pradeep said.

"Does that mean they're here?" I asked, grabbing my backpack to keep Frankie close.

"No, they could upload remotely," Pradeep answered. "But—"

But I interrupted Pradeep's "but." "Frankie's gone!" I held up the backpack. "He must have rolled away while we were looking at the website."

"So now we have two evil big brothers and a zombie goldfish on the loose to worry about," said Pradeep. "What else could go wrong . . . ?"

"Pradeep, my lovely, you forgot your lunch this morning."

Mrs. Kumar's voice filled the school hallway and I watched Pradeep's face fall so low, he had to pick his chin up from the floor.

"Anything but that . . ." he sighed.

# CHAPTER 5

# RETURN OF THE ZOMBIE TODDLER

As I ran over to the classroom door to see where Pradeep's mom was, Pradeep hid under the computer table.

Fair enough, really. Parents coming into school when they are not expected is top of the list of the five most embarrassing things that can happen to a kid in elementary school.

5. The school nurse finds something in your hair, but can't exactly tell what it is, so says, out loud to the rest of the class, "I'm going to have to take a picture of this one and look it up." (Me—third grade.)

4. Your mom mixes up your swimsuit with your little sister's, so you have the choice to go out to the pool stark naked or wearing a three-year-old's Dora the Explorer bikini bottoms. (Pradeep—last year.)

3. You admit, in front of the other boys in your class, that you think the best *Star Wars* movie is the one with the cute, furry little Ewok creatures. (This kid called Ben—just before winter break. He never came back to school.)

2. Your pet zombie goldfish gets loose in the school. (Me—today.)

And 1. Your mom calls you "precious," "lovely," or "honey" in a loud voice in the school hallway just as everyone is coming out of assembly. (Pradeep—also today.)

I peeked around the door and saw Mrs. Kumar looking into the classroom across the corridor. Kids were sniggering as they walked past and

I could hear whispers of "Isn't that Pradeep's mom?"

"Come along, Samina," Mrs. Kumar called, gently pulling Pradeep's little sister by the hand. "We'll have to take Pradeep's lunch to the office."

Mr. Swanson came into the computer lab, followed by loads of kids, so Pradeep had to get out from under the table.

"Tom, they're still online," Pradeep said as he sat up at the desk. "If we can track down which computer in the school they're using, then maybe we can shut the website down."

Pradeep's hands tapped away at the keyboard at the speed of light.

"I got 'em!" Pradeep said. "They're in the science lab upstairs."

"That's not fair," I said. "That's where Mark told us he was going to be and he usually lies so that's the last place I would look."

"Actually, when you think of it that way, it's pretty clever," said Pradeep. Then we looked at each other. "Must have been Sanj's idea," we both said together.

"I'll head up and recon what they're doing in the lab," I said to Pradeep. "We'll keep in contact with clicks." There's a button on our walkie-talkies for tapping out Morse code. Pradeep and I haven't actually learned the real Morse code yet, so we do two different tunes with the clicks to say how things are going. If everything is fine, we click:

SHORT SHORT LONG,
SHORT SHORT LONG,
SHORT SHORT SHORT SHORT LONG (TO
    THE TUNE OF "JINGLE BELLS" 'CAUSE
    IT'S A HAPPY SONG).

If it's an emergency, we click:

LONG SHORT,
LONG SHORT,
SHORT SHORT LONG LONG (TO THE

END BIT OF "RING AROUND THE ROSIE" 'CAUSE IT SEEMS LIKE A HAPPY SONG, BUT IT'S REALLY ABOUT THE PLAGUE. WHICH WAS A PRETTY MAJOR EMERGENCY).

I got another bathroom pass from Mr. Swanson (he must have thought I had serious bladder problems) and headed out into the hall. Just as I reached the staircase, I heard a familiar voice.

"Swishy little fishy," Sami chanted as she skipped along the hallway in front of Pradeep's mom.

I looked at Sami. Her eyes stared through the display board on the wall and up my left nostril. The zombie stare. Frankie had hypnotized Sami again, so he must be close by.

"Ah, Tom," Mrs. Kumar said. "The secretary told me that Pradeep would be in one of these classrooms up here doing computer things. Do you know which one? I've brought his lunch."

Sami was
holding
Pradeep's
teddy-bear
lunchbox—
the one he
keeps trying to
lose or destroy
and his mom

keeps finding and fixing. He
even let the school bus run over it, but it still
didn't break. I bet in a thousand years' time
archaeologists will find Pradeep's teddy-bear
lunchbox still intact, with his mom's super-
plastic-wrapped samosas inside.

Sami opened the lunchbox's lid just a crack
and there inside, swimming around in his
plastic bag, was Frankie. I quickly slammed the
lid shut.

"Um, I can take the lunchbox to him," I said,
trying to grab it from Sami.

"Swishy fishy." She pouted and held on tight to the handle.

"OK, maybe Sami can bring the lunchbox," I said, loud enough so that Frankie would hear me and use his hypnotic powers to control Sami. Just then I saw a flash of white as someone passed behind Mrs. Kumar. It was Mark, still in his Evil Scientist coat.

"Mark!" I shouted, but he'd already run up the stairs.

The lunchbox started to shake back and forth in Sami's hands. Oh great, Frankie had heard Mark's name and was probably now in full green-eyed revenge mode.

"Here, let me hold that, Sami," I said, peeking inside the lid as she let me take it from her. Frankie's eyes were bright green and his tail whacked hard against the sides of the bag.

"Why are you shaking Pradeep's lunch?" Mrs. Kumar asked.

"Um, that's the way Pradeep likes it." I smiled

nervously. "Come on, Sami, let's get this to Pradeep while it's still . . . freshly . . . shook."

Sami looked starey-eyed at me but followed as I headed for the stairs. "I'll bring Sami back down to the office after we find Pradeep," I called to Mrs. Kumar.

We ran up the stairs. Mark must have headed for the science lab. Sami, Frankie, and I would

trick Mark and Sanj into chasing after us, then Pradeep could sneak into the lab and wipe the website, stopping BBEDLAM in its tracks. And all before our first class was over. This was going to be easy. I handed Sami the lunchbox as I opened the science-lab door.

As soon as we stepped inside I knew it was a trap. Mostly because a big mosquito net fell from the ceiling and trapped us. Sami dropped the lunchbox as she fell and it skidded across the floor. I heard Mark's Evil Scientist laugh: "Mwhahahahahahaha! Ha—suckers!"

# CHAPTER 6

# THE DASTARDLY TRAP

Mark and Sanj stepped out from behind the door.

"Everything has gone exactly to plan." Sanj clapped with excitement. "We lied our way into your pathetic little school, we tricked you into bringing the fish with you this morning, we made it so easy for my little moron brother to find our website, and then we tricked you into following Mark up here."

"Yeah, suckers!" Mark said again.

"And now you are our prisoner." Sanj paused. "Oh, hi, Sami," he added.

"Swishy little fishy," Sami said, wriggling under the net.

"Yes, exactly. So where is the fish?" Sanj said.

I stared at Sanj but said nothing.

"Moron, where's the fish?" Mark grunted and kicked my leg.

"I won't tell," I said. Just then the lunchbox started crashing around on its own on the floor, steadily bumping toward Mark.

"I think we found it," said Sanj, reaching down and lifting Frankie's plastic bag out from the lunchbox.

Sanj handed the bag to Mark and picked up his laptop. Frankie was flipping his tail wildly back and forth and his eyes were glow-in-the-dark green. Mark put on his Evil Scientist

protective goggles and glared at Frankie. Frankie glared back, harder.

Then Mark turned to Sanj. "So you got it?" he asked, taking off his goggles.

"Yes, thank you, that was sufficient," Sanj answered.

"Cool. Now we got the zombie stare!" Mark said, tapping the little webcam attached to the side of his goggles. "Wicked! Now I can do whatever I want to the fish, right?" he added, dumping Frankie out of his bag and into a glass beaker that was sitting on top of an unlit Bunsen burner, next to a row of test tubes filled with colored liquid.

"Don't hurt him!" I shouted from under the net, struggling to break free.

"The moron is right for now," Sanj said. "Let's see if the plan works first before you dispose of the fish. The computer class will all be looking at their screens, so I'll test BBEDLAM's zombie fish-stare hypno-virus on them."

Sanj hit some buttons on his computer and an image streamed onto the whiteboard in the science lab. He must have set up a secret camera in the computer lab. You could see the back of Mr. Swanson's head and then all the kids in front of him, looking at their computers.

"Sanj, Pradeep is in there. What will it do to him?" I said.

"Let's see." Sanj smiled an evil smile and hit "send."

I watched the whiteboard. The millipedes and cockroaches were now using my stomach as a bouncy castle.

I didn't know what was going to happen, but I knew it wouldn't be good. Pradeep was right at the back of the classroom, so I couldn't see his face very well, but all the other kids were sitting at their screens and staring like . . . zombies. Then Pradeep's mom walked into the room and started talking to Mr. Swanson. But as soon as she glanced at a computer screen she immediately stared at the wall and up Mr. Swanson's left nostril. Mr. Swanson was clearly zombified too.

Sami looked at the image of her mom on the whiteboard. "Swishy fishy mommy," she chanted.

"I think you're right, Sami," I whispered.

"Mom?" Sanj said, surprised. "Oh well, that will keep her out of the way."

"Result!" Mark said and punched the air. Then he looked confused. "That's what it was supposed to do—right, Sanj?"

"Yes, it works perfectly. We can upload the zombie hypno-virus onto any computer, and whoever looks at the screen will instantly be hypnotized into being our zombie fish slave. Then we can program them to do whatever we want!" Sanj attempted an evil laugh, but it came out more like a gasping wheeze.

Mark did an absolutely flawless evil laugh. You have to give it to him. Sanj might have smarter plans, but Mark's got the evil laugh down.

"So *now* can I do what I want to the fish?" Mark said.

Just then I heard a crash of breaking glass. Frankie had knocked the beaker off the tripod and was surfing in the rush of water across the lab bench. His eyes glowed a perfect shade of revenge green.

"Stupid moron fish!" Mark shouted, and clambered over the bench toward Frankie.

Frankie dodged Mark's hands as they tried to flatten him. The wave was rolling in one direction—toward the sink at the end of the bench.

"No!" I shouted.

"Swishy little fishy," Sami squealed.

Mark ran to the sink and held out his hands to catch the fish. But Frankie leaped into the air, thwacked Mark around the face with his tail, did a perfect somersault, and dived directly down the drain. If there were an Olympic event in Zombie Fish Diving, he so would have won the gold!

"Moron fish!" Mark thumped the bench with his fist. "Oww!" he said, and rubbed his hand.

"Oh, get over it, Mark. We have bigger fish to fry." Sanj smiled at his own joke but Mark just looked confused. "Bigger FISH to fry," repeated Sanj. Still no reaction. "Oh, never mind." He sighed. "Now we need to keep these two here so they don't mess up Stage Two of BBEDLAM's plan."

"What's Stage Two?" Mark and I said at exactly the same time.

"Turning the whole school into fish-stare zombie slaves. Keep up," Sanj said. "All the little

moron brothers and sisters will do whatever
I tell them to. Then, who knows, maybe I'll
just upload the Zombie Goldfish Virus on the
Internet. Soon there'll be fish-stare zombies
everywhere." Sanj paused again. "Now would be
a good time for your evil laugh, Mark."

"I'm not in the mood," Mark grumped. "I
want to hurt that fish and I'm gonna search this
school until I find him." He stormed off.

"Whatever. I don't need you anyway." Sanj
picked up his laptop. "Now I'm going to have a
chat with the principal. I'll be back in a second
so don't go anywhere." Sanj attempted an
evil laugh, but it just came out wheezy again.
"Ahem, ahem." He pretended he was clearing his
throat and then followed Mark out of the lab.

Sami was still looking over at the sink. "Swishy
fishy gone?" she mumbled. With Frankie gone,
Sami came out of her trance. She didn't look
fish-starey anymore, just kind of sad.

"Frankie will be OK, Sami, as long as we find

him before Mark does," I said. "I'm more worried about Pradeep."

What if my best friend was now a zombie fish slave?

# CHAPTER 7

# TSUNAMI ZOMBIE TROUBLE

I took my compass and protractor out of my pocket and used them to cut a hole in the net. I'm not sure what you're actually supposed to use them for, but they're pretty handy for poking holes in stuff. And I never thought I would be so grateful for math equipment.

I freed Sami and we both headed straight down to the computer room. Everyone was still and silent, and totally zombified. Sami ran up to her mom.

"Swishy fishy mommy." She tugged on her mom's skirt, but Mrs. Kumar didn't move.

Then, from my walkie-talkie I heard some clicks:

SHORT SHORT LONG,
SHORT SHORT LONG,
SHORT SHORT SHORT SHORT LONG.

It was "Jingle Bells"! "Pradeep, where are you?" I whispered, looking around the classroom.

"Under here," Pradeep whispered back. Sami and I ran to his desk and found him hiding underneath it.

"We thought you'd been zombified," I said.

Sami crawled under the desk and hugged Pradeep. "Ahh. Not swishy fishy," she said.

"I ducked under the desk when Mom came in," explained Pradeep, "so I missed whatever it was that did this to them. I swear I saw a close-up picture of Frankie's eyes on the screen before I jumped under the desk."

"Sanj and Mark figured out a way to turn Frankie's zombie stare into a computer virus," I told him. "They tested it on the computer class and now they're going to zombify the whole

school and then the whole world!"

"Wow, they *are* thinking big." Pradeep paused. "OK, if it's our big brothers who are going to try to take over the world, then I guess it's up to us to stop them."

We high-fived. *It was the kind of moment that called for a high five*, I thought.

"So, where are Sanj and Mark now?" Pradeep asked. "And where's Frankie?"

"Sanj has gone to find Mrs. Prentice, to zombify her, I think, and Frankie is somewhere in the water pipes. He escaped down a drain! Mark is trying to find him—he's probably checking every sink and toilet in the school."

We heard footsteps in the hall and then Sanj's voice, along with Mrs. Prentice's. I dropped down under the desk with Sami and Pradeep.

"Does Sanj think I was zombified?" Pradeep whispered.

I nodded.

"Then I can go undercover and see what he's

going to do. No one will suspect a fish zombie," he said, and then slowly sat back up in his chair.

I tugged on Pradeep's pant leg and when he looked down at me I did zombie eyes at him to remind him to put on the stare. He immediately started staring up Susan Renwick's left nostril and at the wall. Pradeep is a pro.

Sanj, in his best "innocent voice," said to Mrs. Prentice, "I'm not sure what happened. I think it was something on Mr. Swanson's computer that he was reading. Have a look." Sanj turned the computer screen to face Mrs. Prentice and pushed a button on the keyboard. In a second Mrs. Prentice was mumbling, "Swishy little fishy."

"This is just too easy," Sanj said, and did his

sinister wheeze again. "Now come with me, Mrs. Prentice, and all you lovely fishy zombies. We're going to the hall to make an announcement to the school."

Pradeep stood up and joined the line of zombie kids following Sanj.

"We'll take care of Mark and find Frankie," I whispered. "You try and stop Sanj."

Sami and I waited until everyone had left the room before we came out from under the desk. Just as we got to the door of the classroom we heard a flush. Then another, then another, then another. Then the cry of, "I'll find you, Fish! You can't hide from me!"

"Mark," Sami and I said together. We peeked around the corner into the hallway. The boys' bathroom was next door. That's where Mark was, which meant Frankie was probably nearby too.

OK, there were three reasons why I couldn't take Sami in the boys' bathroom with me:

1. Mark was in there, and possibly Frankie, and with the two of them together that was not going to be pretty.

2. There are standing-up boys' toilets in there and I don't want to explain to a three-year-old girl what they are for.

3. The boys' bathroom is the one place in school that a guy can feel totally sure that he's never ever going to see a girl. If I brought Sami in, then I think I would be breaking a sacred code for all boykind.

"Sami, I need to send you somewhere safe while I go and help Frankie," I said. But where was free from computers or whiteboards or anything that could zombify Sami with the virus? Then it came to me. Well, my stomach growled, which made me think I was hungry, which made me think of food, which made me think of lunch, which made me think of the cafeteria . . . Bingo! The one place in the school with no screens of any

kind. The one place Sami would be safe.

"Go and hide in the cafeteria, Sami. I'll find you there. It's just down these stairs and around the corner." She didn't seem to want to go. "They have cookies down there," I added. Sami skipped off down the stairs. "Shhhh," I whispered after her.

"Shhhhishy fisshhhhhhy," she echoed back up the stairwell.

I snuck into the bathroom and hid behind the door. Mark was turning on all the taps one by one. Just as he got to the last sink and turned the tap, Frankie burst out of the pipe in a whoosh of water, flipped in the air over Mark's head, then over one of the stalls, and plopped into the toilet bowl. "Now I got you, Fish," Mark said, and an Evil Scientist creepy smile spread across his face.

Mark ran to flush the toilet, but Frankie leaped to the next one just in time. You could see flashes of Frankie's green eyes and gold fins as he dived over the stalls. Mark just missed flushing him every time. When he reached the last toilet, Frankie leaped back over to the sinks again. The water was still running out of all the taps. Frankie landed in the first sink and Mark ran toward him with a plastic bag. Frankie tried to escape down the drain, but Mark had blocked the sinks with balled-up paper towels. They were filling up to overflowing and Frankie was desperately hopping back and forth between them, trying to avoid being scooped up by Mark. I had to save Frankie.

# CHAPTER 8

# NINJA ZOMBIE SHOWDOWN

"Leave Frankie alone!" I shouted at Mark. I tried to grab his arm, but water was spilling from the sinks so that when Mark pushed me, I went sliding across the floor and whacked against the shower stall in the corner. The shower stall that had a drain in its floor that meant Frankie could get out!

"Frankie! Over here!" I yelled, lifting up the grate that blocked the drain.

Frankie's eyes burned a fiercer green. He propelled himself out of the sink using all his strength. As Frankie jumped he was facing the mirrors above the sink, but he was at eye level with Mark—just for a second. His stare met Mark's reflection and Mark suddenly looked over to the wall and toward my nostril. Frankie was hypnotizing him! But he suddenly dropped to the floor, breaking eye contact. Still, it was enough to stun him.

Frankie let the overflowing water carry him across the tiles and toward the drain. He flicked his tail in a wave to me as he passed by, and then he was down the drain and away from Mark.

"Arnnmmrrggg," Mark moaned. He was coming out of his stunned zombified state. I had to get out of there. I scrambled across the wet floor and ran out the door.

As I got to the top of the stairs, an announcement came over the loudspeaker. It was Mrs. Prentice's voice, but she sounded weird. "Would all students and teachers please tune in to the internal school channel on the whiteboards or computers. We are now going to show a mandatory video about Internet safety. Everyone must watch." I heard Sanj's sinister wheeze in the background. This was it. Sanj was going to hypnotize everyone in the school. I crossed my fingers and hoped that Pradeep could stop him in time. I knew Frankie was OK for now. I had to get Sami and go and help Pradeep.

As I tiptoed into the cafeteria in the basement, I could hear Sami's voice. I poked my head around the kitchen door and saw her sitting on one of the kitchen counters, with the lunch ladies gathered around. Oh no! What if they were zombie lunch ladies?! I was just about to jump out from behind the door and surprise the zombie lunch ladies when I heard Sami singing, "One, two, three, four, five, once I caught fishy alive . . ."

The lunch ladies all clapped. Good. They were distracted, now was my best chance for a rescue.

I pounced into the room doing my best ninja stance. "Hiiiii-ya!" I shouted. "I'm here, Sami, I'll save you!"

They all turned to look at me. At first they gave me the classic lunch-lady stare. The stare that said, "Don't you even ask me what's in this

lunch because
you don't want
to know and
anyway I'd
have to kill you
if I told you."

Then the
lunch lady with
the orange hairnet
smiled and said,
"Oh, this is the little boy whose brother ate his
egg this morning. Remember? I told you." Then
they all smiled and shared a look.

"Oh, yes, poor thing," one said. They nodded
sympathetically.

"So have you come to collect our little princess
here?" the orange-hairnet lunch lady said as
she lifted Sami off the counter. "She wandered
in saying something about a fishy so I asked her
if she knew any songs about fishies and she just
started singing. You're a good little singer, aren't

you?" she said, patting Sami on the head. The other lunch ladies nodded.

Sami looked at me and giggled.

I was stunned. I had never heard a lunch lady say anything but "More egg?" to me ever. They always looked so scary, but these ones seemed nice. And even better, they weren't fish zombies.

"Excuse me, ma'am?" I said.

"Oh, isn't he so polite? Not like some of them," one of the lunch ladies said. They all nodded again.

"Have any of you looked at a computer this morning?" I asked.

"We don't need a computer down here, honey," the hairnet lunch lady answered. "Why?"

I thought about explaining that my Evil Scientist big brother and Pradeep's Evil Computer Genius big brother had formed an evil society called BBEDLAM that had taken over the school's computers and, right now, they were

planning on turning all the students and staff into fish zombies. But then I changed my mind.

Another announcement came over the loudspeaker. "Everyone seems to be online, so we'll start the program. I'm uploading the virus—I mean the *safety video* now," Sanj said with the robot voice effect he had before. "Keep watching your screens until the film ends."

After a few seconds I heard the creepy sound of hundreds of students and teachers all mumbling, "Swishy little fishy." Too late to stop the school from being zombified now. But I could still stop it happening to us and the rest of the world.

"Your first command, my zombie fish slaves," continued Sanj, "is find that little moron Tom—"

"And his moron fish," Mark interrupted.

"And his moron fish," Sanj repeated. "Then bring them to me."

# CHAPTER 9

# BATTLE OF THE UNDEAD FISH ZOMBIES

"Is this something to do with the school play?" one of the lunch ladies asked. "Is it about zombies this year? Seems a bit inappropriate for an elementary school if you ask me." The other lunch ladies nodded again.

"Are you Tom?" the orange-hairnet lunch lady asked. I nodded this time. "I'm Gladys," she said. "Hope you don't mind my saying, but this sounds like trouble."

"This might sound really weird, but I think there will be lots of hypnotized fish-starey zombies heading down here looking for us. We have to go." I grabbed Sami's hand.

"I think you'll be all right down here. They never remember us lunch ladies. Probably forgot we even exist," said Gladys, her smile fading a little bit.

"It'll be better if Sami and I leave," I said.

I grabbed a serving tray and a spatula from the counter, as I figured we might have to protect ourselves against fish-starey zombies, and led Sami back into the hallway. We ran straight into Madame Bouvard, the French teacher. She was lurching toward us mumbling, *"Le swishy petit poisson, le swishy petit poisson . . ."*

I pushed Sami behind me and held

up the tray to block Madame Bouvard's swinging arm. She stopped. She stared at her reflection in the shiny metal surface and started to moan, like Mark had done in the boys' bathroom when Frankie hypnotized him. It seemed that, somehow, seeing their own zombie stare reflected back stunned the fish zombies. This could be a way to fight them off!

We ran back into the kitchen and pulled Gladys to one side. "I've got a plan, but we need all the lunch ladies to help." Gladys looked confused now.

I tried to explain. "We need to use the shiny metal food trays to reflect the zombie goldfish stares back at the kids and teachers who've been zombified."

"I always said those trays were clean enough to see yourself in," Gladys said with pride, "but I'm not sure how the other lunch ladies will cope. It won't be good for Betty's blood pressure and Carol was just saying that she

felt a migraine coming on."

I looked at Sami and then at Gladys. *We can't do this on our own*, I thought. We need a secret weapon.

Just then the pipes above the sink started gurgling and then the tap turned. Frankie shot out in a swoosh of water, landing in the big stainless steel sink. The other lunch ladies screamed. Gladys shouted, "Quiet, ladies! Haven't you ever seen a fish in a kitchen before?"

Frankie jumped out of the sink and into a pitcher of orange Kool-Aid that was on the counter. I picked up the jug. "Frankie, you're OK!" I said, so relieved to see him. Frankie swished his tail against my hand to give me a fishy high five.

Then I heard footsteps on the ceiling above us. Lots of footsteps. The zombies must have heard the lunch ladies' screams. I ran over to the kitchen doors and shoved a broomstick between

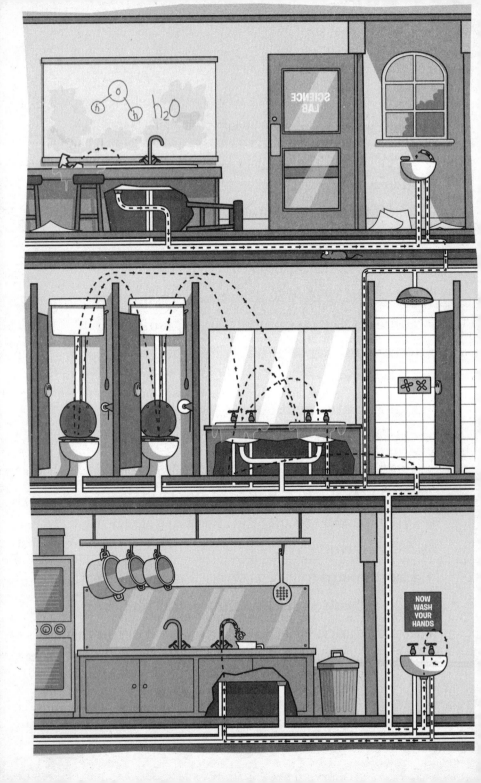

the handles to block the door. The lunch ladies stared at me.

"I saw them do it once on TV," I said, and they nodded.

Sami squeezed my hand. Frankie's eyes were bright green now and he thrashed around wildly. Gladys peered into the jug.

"Don't look him in the eye," I warned, "or else you'll get the zombie stare, like all the fish zombies upstairs. Only a little better, because if Frankie hypnotizes you, then *he* can control what you do, and not BBEDLAM." She started to look confused again.

"So the goldfish can zombie people too, but in a good way?" she said.

Then a giant searchlight went off inside my head, pointing at the lightbulb with a single brilliant idea.

"Yes! That's what Frankie can do. And that's exactly what *we* should do!" I shouted. "You're a genius, Gladys!"

I carried Frankie over to the other lunch ladies and asked them to look into his eyes until they were all zombified. Now Frankie could control them (without increasing Betty's blood pressure or giving Carol a migraine, or freaking any of them out any more than they already were). I whispered the plan to Frankie, about bouncing back the zombie stare with the trays and then re-hypnotizing the zombies to bring them under his control. He made all the lunch ladies pick up shiny metal trays and get ready for battle.

The footsteps had reached the stairs and there was banging on the cafeteria doors. For all I knew, Pradeep could be a zombie by now. I lifted Frankie's jug up to Gladys so she could get zombified too.

"Don't be silly," she said. "Someone has to keep their wits about them. Besides, I've seen more zombie films than you've had hot lunches. Never look them in the eye. Never surrender."

She winked at me and held up her silver tray like
a shield.

Suddenly the fish zombies came bursting
through the kitchen doors, all chanting, "Swishy
little fishy."

One by one, the lunch ladies used their trays
to stun them. Then I ran over with Frankie so
he could zombify them again. Slowly we were
getting more of the kids and teachers on our side

and they were picking up trays and joining the fight.

My walkie-talkie started to click:

**LONG SHORT,
LONG SHORT,
SHORT SHORT LONG LONG,**

**LONG SHORT,
LONG SHORT,
SHORT SHORT LONG LONG.**

It went on that long because I didn't have a hand free to answer it. I handed Frankie's jug to Sami.

Pradeep was clicking "Ring Around the Rosie," which meant . . . he was in big trouble.

# CHAPTER 10

# DAWN OF THE LUNCH LADIES

"We've got to help Pradeep!" I shouted to Gladys as she held up two trays and stunned both the school secretaries at once.

"Who?" she asked.

"Choc-Rice-Pops-on-toast boy!" I answered.

"Oh, I worry about his diet," she sighed. "Go— and take little princess with you. We'll keep stunning these zombies till you get back with the goldfish."

I looked around. There was no way we could get past the fish zombies and escape up the stairs. Mr. Walker, the PE teacher, was taking up the whole doorway, and none of the lunch ladies was tall enough to un-zombie him. I had to get to Pradeep. Then I spotted the tiny door behind the kitchen counter.

"What's that?" I asked Gladys.

"Oh, that's an old dumbwaiter from years back. When they used to have big events in the hall upstairs, they used that to send up trays and plates and things."

I opened the little door. It was small but just big enough for Sami to fit in. At least I could get her out safely, and then I'd have to run the gauntlet of fish zombies and hope for the best. I helped Sami crawl into the little elevator. At first she clung to my hand, but she let go when I handed her the jug with Frankie inside.

"You take Frankie upstairs and I'll come and find you," I said. I closed the door and pulled the ropes to hoist her up. I could hear a muffled "Wheeeee!" as she rose in the tiny elevator.

Now I just had to get past Mr. Walker. I had to out-PE the PE teacher. I ran toward him and ducked left, ducked right, and then dived between his legs and out the other side. Yes! I swerved out of the reach of Mrs. Fletcher, the librarian, and then leaped past the Mackenzie twins. This was just like playing *Zombie Hero Defender* on the computer, but with lots of "swishy fishy" chanting instead of cool laser-blasting sound effects.

I raced up the stairs and ran along the hallway to the assembly hall, where the dumbwaiter comes out. I opened the little hatch but it was empty. No Sami. No Frankie.

The giant whiteboard in the assembly hall booted up again. A voice came out of the speakers: "Hey! Moron!" It was Mark this time. "Guess who just dropped in to see us?"

An image flickered onto the whiteboard. It showed Sami wedged into the science lab trash can. That kid has a bad habit of getting stuck in trash cans. Then the camera panned up and across. There was Frankie in his plastic jug of

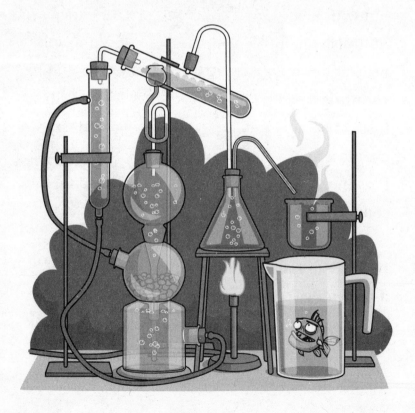

orange Kool-Aid. Above him was a whole series of bubbling test tubes and glass pipes carrying glowing green liquid. The liquid was bubbling up in a beaker at the end and when it reached the top it would spill over—onto Frankie.

The camera turned to Sanj, sitting at his laptop. He was looking straight into the lens. "I've now set the countdown clock. In exactly five minutes the BBEDLAM Zombie Fish Virus will upload onto the Internet. Then it will spread to every computer worldwide and everyone will see that I'm more gifted than anyone at that stupid gifted school." He did his sinister wheeze. "Just try and stop me, little moron!" he added.

# CHAPTER 11

# NO ONE SUSPECTS
# A ZOMBIE

Just then some kid fish zombies staggered into the hall, and Pradeep was one of them.

As they got closer I could see he had a zombified Darren Schultz on his left and the zombified Mackenzie twins on his right. There was no way I could take them all. If only I had a mirror . . . I ran to the door and headed to the boys' bathroom. The zombies followed me. I stood in front of the mirrors as the zombies got closer. Darren was the first one to stand still, stunned. Then the Mackenzie twins stopped too. Pradeep looked to his left and right.

"Oh, I see you reversed the effects of the

zombie stare by forcing eye contact with the opposite mirror reflection. That's cool, Tom," Pradeep said.

"Is that what I'm doing?" I said. "Hey, wait, you're not a fish zombie after all."

"No, I was looking for you to warn you about Sanj putting the virus on the Internet when Darren and the twins followed me. I couldn't blow my cover or they would have taken me prisoner."

"We have to get up to the science lab, Pradeep," I said. "They've got Frankie and Sami!"

"On the double," Pradeep said, already heading for the stairs.

When we got to the science lab, I looked over at the countdown clock on Sanj's laptop: 02:43. There were only two minutes and forty-three seconds left to stop them.

Pradeep winked at me outside the door and then put on his zombie stare. He grabbed me by the arms and pulled me into the room.

"Swishy little fishy," he droned.

"Moron!" Mark yelled. "Awesome. And you're too late. Ha! The fish is about to be toxic toast."

"And you get to see my computer virus released on the world in two minutes and eleven seconds," Sanj said.

Pradeep staggered nearer to Frankie, holding me tight like I was his prisoner. I pretended to struggle.

Sami looked over at us as she tried to squirm out of the trash can. She smiled at me and then stuck her tongue out at Pradeep, blowing a raspberry. "Ptbblllllllllbbbbbbbbbbllllbbbbbb! Naughty Pradeep," she said.

Sanj grinned at me. "I think it's so fitting that my stupid little moron brother, your little moron best friend, is the one who turned you in. It's just so sad. I mean, he didn't even put up a fight or anything. . . ." Sanj babbled on and didn't even notice that Pradeep was zombie-walking over to the laptop cord, which was hanging over the other side of the table. Pradeep slowly reached out and yanked the cord, pulling the laptop out of Sanj's reach and into his own hands.

"Stupid little moron, huh?" Pradeep said and started typing. "Then how come I memorized your super-long 'un-hackable' password just by watching you type it? Now I can shut this thing down." Pradeep's fingers flew over the keyboard. Mark and Sanj both raced to stop him.

I grabbed Frankie's plastic jug and threw it

at Mark. It clocked him right on the side of the head and knocked him off balance. He turned back to me. "You just did my job for me, moron, getting rid of the fish! Now I'll get rid of you."

# CHAPTER 12
# ZOMBIE VIRUS COUNTDOWN

Sanj snatched the computer from Pradeep's hands and pushed him to the floor. You know, it is so unfair that no matter how much we outsmart our evil big brothers, they are still two feet taller and usually able to squash us if they want to. I watched Pradeep getting squashed and knew my own squashing was just a matter of time. "Forty-five seconds left and still five numbers to enter on my password code," Sanj gloated. "There's no way to stop me now. I'll have a whole world of zombie fish slaves! You lose, I win, na-na na-na-na."

"And you *so* lose!" Mark said as he caught up

with me and grabbed me around my arms so I couldn't move.

I looked Mark right in the eye, and that's when I released my secret weapon. I opened my mouth and Frankie jumped out, slapping his tail hard across Mark's face until he fell backward into the mosquito net I'd been trapped under earlier. I quickly rolled the net around him as Frankie fell to the floor and skidded along its watery surface, skating toward Sanj.

"Look out, Frankie!" Pradeep yelled as Sanj

stomped his feet, trying to squash Frankie. But Frankie bounced off the top of Sanj's boot, leaped over his head and landed on the laptop.

Ten seconds, read the clock. Frankie flipped around on the keyboard, thwacking keys with his tail and dodging Sanj's fist. The clock ticked on:

7 . . .

6 . . .

5 . . .

Thwack, thwack, thwack on the keys.

4 . . .

3 . . .

2 . . .

Tap tap, tap.

1 . . .

And then it froze.

Sanj stared at the screen. "Impossible," he said. "How could a fish type in code?" Sanj collapsed on the floor talking to himself.

"Yeah, you'd have to be a stupid little moron to be outwitted by a couple of little kids and a fish," I said. "Right, Frankie?"

That's when I saw the goldfish.

"Fishy not swishy?!" Sami struggled in the trash can, pointing to Frankie lying motionless on the laptop keyboard.

"No, Frankie, you can't!" I said. "Quick, we need to get him in some water!"

Pradeep ran to get the jug off the floor and filled it from the tap.

I gently placed Frankie in the water as Pradeep

pulled Sami out of the trash can. She hugged him around the knees.

Sanj was still mumbling to himself on the floor. "How could he do that? How could the fish figure it out?"

Sami toddled over to Sanj and dumped the trash can on his head. "Naughty Sanj!" she said.

The lunch ladies who Frankie had hypnotized burst into the science lab with Gladys right behind them. "I don't know what they're doing," she said. "Betty just put some eggs on a plate and Carol grabbed a moldy bread roll and they headed up here. We've stunned all the teachers and students now anyway. Although nobody can reach Mr. Walker. Ethel and Mildred have him cornered behind the salad bar—"

"I think Frankie must have summoned them somehow," I interrupted, "and sent them a message with what he needs. Look!"

"Oh, he doesn't look good, does he? Poor fish. Looks famished. No wonder he wanted eggs and bread, but why the moldy ones?"

"They're green!" Pradeep and I said at the same time. I realized I talk at the same time as a lot of people. Gotta work on that. I checked no one else was about to speak before I added, "He only likes green food."

I took the eggs and moldy rolls and crumbled them into the jug. Frankie shook slightly, then his mouth opened and closed. He started gobbling up egg bits and moldy bread. He looked up at me from his jug, winked, and swished his tail.

"Good to have you back, Frankie," I said, patting him gently on his top fin. "We just need your help with one more thing," I added, before Pradeep and I whispered the next stage of our plan.

# CHAPTER 13
# FIN-TASTIC FINALE

We tied Sanj in the mosquito netting too and
let Frankie zombify him and Mark so they
wouldn't try to escape. Then we went down
to the basement and Frankie re-zombied the
BBEDLAM-stunned zombies, so that they were
under his control. He made them all go to the
assembly hall, including the lunch ladies and
Mrs. Kumar. Pradeep and I wrote a message on
the whiteboard that said: "Welcome to the Lunch
Lady Appreciation Assembly."

Frankie released everyone from his control
and they all blinked to life. The zombie-stares
had vanished.

"It's like they've been rebooted," Pradeep said.

On cue, Pradeep and Sami and I started singing, "For they are jolly good ladies, for they are jolly good ladies, for they are jolly good ladies, which nobody can deny!" And everyone just kind of joined in. The lunch ladies looked surprised and some of them even blushed. Gladys smiled bigger than ever.

Mrs. Prentice looked confused to find herself standing at the microphone at the front of the assembly hall. She read the whiteboard and looked over at the beaming faces of the lunch ladies and said, "Yes, um, of course, the school couldn't function without the dedication of our much-valued catering staff."

"Three cheers for the lunch ladies!" I shouted.

The whole hall replied, "Hip, hip, hooray! Hip, hip, hooray! Hip, hip, hooray!"

When the assembly was over, we told Mrs. Prentice that we had found the purple-traitors

(even though neither of them was wearing purple) of the false fire alarm and computer prank and that they were in the science lab. Pradeep and I ran ahead, and Pradeep wiped the virus off Sanj's laptop just in time.

Mark and Sanj were still tied up when Mrs. Prentice and Mrs. Kumar walked in.

"Stupid moron, letting a fish crack your code!" Mark shouted.

"No, you are the stupid moron for not catching the fish in the first place!" Sanj shouted back.

"You are *so* not evil enough to be in my gang," Mark said.

"And you are far too intellectually *inferior* to be in my gang," Sanj replied.

Mark's face looked like his brain was trying to figure out what Sanj just said, then he gave up and thumped Sanj instead. "Whatever!" he grunted.

Mrs. Prentice leaned over Sanj and Mark. "I've spoken to the principal at the middle school,

so you can add truancy to your list of other
misdemeanors, like tampering with the fire
alarm and hacking the school computer."

Basically, Mrs. Prentice was telling them that
they were busted.

"I think you boys have a lot of explaining to
do," she said.

She led the boys toward her office, with Pradeep's mom tutting at Sanj. Then Mrs. Kumar stopped and turned around. "Samina," she called. Sami skipped out of the science lab, carrying Pradeep's lunchbox.

"Oh, thank you, Samina. Here's your lunch, Pradeep." She paused for a second. "Oh, I nearly forgot the way you like it." She gave the lunchbox a shake before handing it to Pradeep.

Pradeep gave me a look that said, "I bet you know why she did that, but I won't ask you now." And I knew exactly what his look meant.

Sami waved as she trotted off after her mom. "Bye, swishy shaky fishy," she giggled.

Pradeep opened the lunchbox—and there was Frankie in the plastic bag that I had put him in after the lunch-lady assembly. The goldfish's eyeballs were spinning around in their bulging sockets.

"Poor Frankie," I said. "I don't think he's

going to want to come to school with me again."

"Hey, Frankie, let's go and see the lunch ladies," Pradeep said.

"Yeah, I bet they could find you something green to eat," I added.

Frankie swished his tail and it even looked like he gave us a fins-up sign with his left fin.

In the cafeteria Gladys said that she would keep our secret about Frankie.

"He's the cutest little zombie fish really," she said. I think Frankie blushed, but it was hard to tell through his fish scales. "Besides, it's the most exciting day at work I've ever had," she carried on, "and don't worry, next time you're in the food line, I'll give you an extra egg." She nudged my arm with her spatula and smiled.

My stomach lurched at the thought, but Frankie thrashed around in excitement. I guess I could always take it home as a treat for him. 'Cause, from now on, Frankie's safer staying at home. I never realized how dangerous school can be. Luckily, we've got a big fat zombie goldfish to help out when things get rough. I wonder how good he is at times tables . . . ?

# ACKNOWLEDGMENTS

I have so many people to thank for taking *My Big Fat Zombie Goldfish* by the fin and leading it to publication.

First I have to thank the volunteers and members of SCBWI (Society of Children's Book Writers and Illustrators). I would never have written this book without the support that SCBWI has given me over the years. I wrote *My Big Fat Zombie Goldfish* for a SCBWI contest run by Sara Grant and Sarah Manson. So thank you so much to both of them.

I also want to thank my friends in my fantastic critique group, Sue Hyams, Paolo Romeo, and Liz De Jager, for cheering me on and cheering me up when I most needed it and for helping my manuscript along its journey.

I want to thank Brady the goldfish (who lives with my amazing agent Gemma Cooper). It's because of Brady that Gemma asked to see the manuscript of *My Big Fat Zombie Goldfish* when we met at an SCBWI conference last year. I of course have to thank Gemma for being everything I could possibly ask for in an agent and a friend and for working with me on the manuscript and making it as strong as it could be before we sent it out to the wide world, where it was hooked by Emma Young and Sam Swinnerton at Macmillan UK and Jean Feiwel at Feiwel and Friends.

I especially have to thank Ruth, Emma, Sam, and the UK team at Macmillan for everything they have done and Jean, Holly, and the team at Feiwel and Friends for encouraging, editing, promoting, and throwing the best Zombie Goldfish suprise party ever.

Lastly, thank you to my friends for believing in me and thank you to my fiancé, Guy, and my kids, Daniel and Charlotte, who have made what could have been a very difficult few years so much fun. Thanks for the coffees and the cuddles.

# Go Fish!

# It's a Zombie Word Scramble—of the fishiest kind

## Can you unscramble these words and find out what they should say?

(If you get stuck, answers are at the bottom of the page.)

1. ifsshy whyis _ _ _ _ _ _ _ _ _ _ _

2. gizmo fish be old _ _ _ _ _ _  _ _ _ _ _ _ _

3. lets visit nice _ _ _ _  _ _ _ _ _ _ _ _

4. freak nest inn _ _ _ _ _ _ _ _ _ _ _ _ _

5. mine expert _ _ _ _ _ _ _ _ _ _

# It's a Zombie Wordsearch

Can you spot these Zombie Goldfish words lurking around? They may be backwards, forwards, up, down or diagonal. Once you've spotted them, put a circle around them, so you don't lose them again.

**EVIL**      **GUNK**      **FISHBOWL**
**SCIENTIST**      **FRANKENSTEIN**      **EXPERIMENT**
**ZOMBIE**      **FREAKY**      **SWISHY FISHY**
**GOLDFISH**      **GREEN**

```
Y  C  P  T  S  I  T  N  E  I  C  S  G
N  H  E  X  P  E  R  I  M  E  N  T  N
S  V  S  T  B  S  V  E  Z  F  W  D  I
W  U  G  I  C  F  G  U  T  R  V  N  E
I  T  U  T  F  R  K  W  I  E  M  K  T
S  A  L  R  E  D  R  N  K  A  G  T  S
H  Z  A  E  X  I  L  V  O  K  B  L  N
Y  U  N  Z  N  H  A  O  Y  Y  W  C  E
F  D  G  O  E  V  I  L  G  O  R  Z  K
I  P  M  W  L  F  D  K  B  X  O  A  N
S  G  U  N  K  B  E  H  V  M  B  L  A
H  A  B  Z  L  T  S  P  B  H  F  T  R
Y  L  D  O  M  I  P  I  H  E  A  M  F
K  Z  I  N  F  H  E  T  L  N  Y  R  I
```

# Spot the Difference

Tom and Pradeep are about to bring Frankie the goldfish back to life with disastrous results! Can you spot the differences between these two images? There are six differences to circle.

# ZOMBIE LIB:
## Bring Your Pet to School Day

"_____" I screamed as I felt a shot of _____
   EXCLAMATION                                        ADJECTIVE
water hit my face.

"Ok, Frankie. I'm up! I'm up!"

I _____ out of bed and put on my _____ .
  ACTION ENDING IN "ED"                              PIECE OF CLOTHING
Today was Bring Your Pet to School Day and it was the first time I had a

pet to bring in. So I was not going to be late.

I ran down the _____ and crunched my _____
                THING IN A HOUSE                         FOOD
for breakfast in _____ seconds flat.
                  NUMBER
Frankie jumped into his _____ and we headed off to school.
                         CONTAINER
When we got there, lots of _____ kids had already arrived.
                            ADJECTIVE
Rachel had brought in her _____ pet _____ .
                           ADJECTIVE              ANIMAL
The _____ fur actually matched her hair!
     COLOR
"Tom, this is _____," she said _____ .
               PET NAME                     ADVERB
Frankie _____ in his _____ .
         ACTION ENDING IN "ED"      SAME CONTAINER
I think he didn't like Rachel's pet that much.

The twins Claudia and Harrison had matching _____ pets.
                                              ANIMAL

Both pets had learned to _____ when the twins shouted
ACTION

_____ at them.
EXCLAMATION

"Wow," was all I could say to that.

Then I saw my friend Deigo. He had a large _____ box that
ADJECTIVE

he was pushing ahead of him.

"You want to meet _____?" he asked.
PET NAME

I started to lift the lid of the _____ box, but whatever was in
ADJECTIVE

the box let out a _____ _____ .
ADVERB              SOUND

"I don't think it wants to meet me," I said.

"She's just _____ sometimes," Deigo answered. "Go ahead."
FEELING / EMOTION

Frankie peaked out of his same container and looked in the

_____ box with me.
ADJECTIVE

Deigo had brought a _____ to school!
EXOTIC ANIMAL

Frankie actually _____ and fin high-fived Deigo's pet.
ACTION ENDING IN "ED"

"I think they'll be friends," I said.

"We should get them some _____ to eat
FOOD

for lunch."

"She's a picky eater," Deigo said. "She only eats

green _____!"
FOOD

"They'll definitely be _____
ADJECTIVE

friends," I said.

# GO FISH

## MO O'HARA

© Aiofetography

**What did you want to be when you grew up?**
When I was a kid, I desperately wanted to be a marine biologist, but I get unbelievably seasick and am terrified of sharks. Not a good combination for a future Jacques Cousteau. So, I settled on being an actor and a writer.

**When did you realize you wanted to be a writer?**
I realized that I got just as much buzz out of someone laughing at something I wrote as I did from something I said. Then, I knew.

**What was your favorite thing about school?**
I loved music class and singing. And reading out loud, too. I always liked being the narrator in assemblies.

**What were your hobbies as a kid?**
Singing, making up stuff, and playing Space Base with my brother. At one point we had taken over the entire basement with a pretend space station made out of cardboard boxes inhabited by *Star Wars* figures and some rogue Barbies. We had very patient parents.

## What are your hobbies now?

Singing (I still love it), making up stuff (even though its part of my job now, it's still fun), and hanging out with my family, but they don't really let me keep lots of cardboard boxes now.

## What was your first job, and what was your "worst" job?

My first job was babysitting. I did a lot of that as a teenager. My worst job was probably dressing up in a full synthetic-fur character suit and waving to kids in 100-degree heat outside a pizza place.

## What book is on your nightstand now?

Kid's book: *Oliver Fibbs and the Giant Boy Munching Bugs* by Steve Hartley. Grown-up book: *Perfect* by Rachel Joyce.

## How did you celebrate publishing your first book?

We had a really fun launch party at a local bookstore, Tales on Moon Lane, and had a big orange cake and green sparkling zombie juice to celebrate (aka prosecco with green food coloring and lemonade with green food coloring for the kids).

## Where do you write your books?

Now, I have a study. (We got a loft extension last year, so it's very new. Yaaaay!) Before that, I wrote on the kitchen table (not literally though, because pen ink is very hard to get out of countertops).

## What sparked your imagination for *My Big Fat Zombie Goldfish*?

When I was a kid, my brother and I brought back a goldfish from the brink of death by shocking him with a 9-volt battery. I had that memory swimming (sorry, bad pun) around in my head for ages, and then a writing competition came up that wanted kids stories based around the Frankenstein story. I called my story "Frankenfish" and wrote the first chapter. Then I asked myself: What if the fish came back wrong? I decided he would work better as a zombie fish and then, as they say, the rest is "fishtory" (sorry, more puns).

### What challenges do you face in the writing process, and how do you overcome them?

I do get writers' block sometimes, and am still terrified of looking at a blank page, but I just keep writing through it. I haven't found an easy way to get over blocks yet, but if I discover it, I'll let you know.

### Which of your characters is most like you?

I'd love to say Sami, but I'm probably a combination of lots of my characters. None of them are all me, though.

### What makes you laugh out loud?

My kids. On a daily basis. I'm very lucky. I get to laugh a lot.

### What do you do on a rainy day?

Go out in the rain.

### What's your idea of fun?

It could be watching a back-to-back *Dr. Who* marathon on TV, riding bikes with the kids, or sitting around with friends, laughing and chatting.

### What is your favorite word?

Mardy. Not as in Mardi Gras or anything. It's a British word from up north and it's such a great word. It sounds just like it means. It's sulky and moody in a grumpy way. Just mardy. It's not really a London word, but I'm totally campaigning to get into use down here, too. Take it across the water and try it out. Go on—move a word across a continent or an ocean, even!

**If you could live in any fictional world, what would it be?**
The Tardis.

**What's your favorite song?**
"Rainbow Connection" by Kermit the Frog (seriously).

**Who is your favorite fictional character?**
Dr. Who (as if you can't guess by now).

**What was your favorite book when you were a kid?**
When I was a little kid, it was *Where the Wild Things Are* by Maurice Sendak. When I was a bit older, it was *Charlie and the Chocolate Factory* by Roald Dahl. And when I was thirteen or so, it became *The Hitchhiker's Guide to the Galaxy* by Douglas Adams.

**Do you have a favorite book now?**
I think I stand by all three of those choices now. Three amazing books.

**What's your favorite TV show or movie?**
Dr. Who (am I coming across as a complete sci-fi geek now? Oh, well).

**If you were stranded on a desert island, who would you want for company?**
My hubby and my kids. Oh, wait . . . all alone, peace and quiet . . . maybe I'd just keep it that way . . . hmm?

**If you could travel anywhere in the world, where would you go and what would you do?**
I'd get a round-the-world ticket and travel all over. Well, anywhere that I didn't have to take a boat to get to (I refer to answer one to your questions).

**If you could travel in time, where would you go and what would you do?**
TARDIS—enough said.

**What's the best advice you have ever received about writing?**
Keep going. Just keep going.

**What do you want readers to remember about your books?**
Friendships, fun, and a fish.

**What would you do if you ever stopped writing?**
I would drive my family nuts with ideas for stories that they should be writing instead.

**If you were a superhero, what would your superpower be?**
I would love to levitate, not even fly really high, just kind of hover around. Oh, or freeze time. That would be cool. Take that, deadlines!

**Do you have any strange or funny habits? Did you when you were a kid?**
I used to be afraid of "the ghost of the bathroom" at my parents' house and had to check behind the shower curtain every time I

went in the bathroom. It's not a problem anymore. We have glass panels in our shower.

**What do you consider to be your greatest accomplishment?**
My kids (although they would insist that they are their own accomplishments, thank you very much) and hopefully connecting with other kids and making them laugh. That is the best feeling in the world.

**What do you wish you could do better?**
Spell.

What happens when a Big Fat Zombie Goldfish meets the Evil Eel of Eel Bay? This is one family vacation that is bound to be . . . electrifying!

Turn the page for a sneak peek of

# MY BIG FAT
# ZOMBIE GOLDFISH
## THE SEAQUEL

# CHAPTER 1

# THE LONG AND WINDING ROAD

Pradeep looked even greener than Frankie's zombie goldfish eyes as we sat in the back of my dad's car. And every time Dad screeched round another bend, Pradeep turned a deeper shade of green. We were on our way to the vacation place that Dad had booked. Usually only Dad, my Evil Scientist big brother Mark, Pradeep's dad and his evil computer-genius big brother Sanj went on the Big Summer Weekend. But this year Sanj was at computer camp, and for the first time Dad said me and Pradeep were old enough to come. Nothing was going to wreck this weekend!

Not Pradeep,
who was just about
to hurl for the fifth
time in four hours (I
could tell because he
had that surprised
look on his face
again). Not Sami,
Pradeep's three-
year-old sister, who
had to come with us
because as soon as

our moms heard Pradeep and I were going away
too, they booked themselves on a Massage and
Mud Pack weekend. (Which I didn't understand
at all. Moms hate mud on your shoes. They
*really* hate mud on the living-room carpet. But
apparently they love it on their faces. Who
knew?) This weekend wouldn't even be ruined
by Mark not saying a word to me since he found
out that Pradeep, Sami, and I were coming. If

only he wouldn't thump me too, then it would be perfect.

"Bag," Pradeep mumbled as we went over a bump in the road.

"Bag," I said to Sami as she bounced in her car seat next to me. She passed me one of the stack of airplane sick bags that Pradeep's mom had packed for him for the journey. I unfolded it and passed it to Pradeep. Pradeep's mom gets these super-strong sick bags off the Internet because they can hold loads without breaking. They make the best splat bombs ever 'cause they never burst until they hit their target. It seemed a shame to waste them on actual car sickness. But a kid's gotta do what a kid's gotta do.

"Bleeech!" Pradeep filled the sick bag and then stared out the window.

"Are we there yet? Are we there yet?" Sami sang from her seat.

Dad looked straight ahead at the winding road. "About twenty minutes maybe," he said.

Pradeep's dad was looking at his smartphone. "It's 13.2 miles exactly to the destination." Pradeep's dad could get a job as one of those GPS things in cars. He's got the perfect voice for it. You would totally believe that he knew where he was going, even if he didn't. I don't think he would fit on the dashboard though.

"If you look toward the sea, you can see the lighthouse from here," Dad said.

Pradeep, Sami, and I all craned our necks to look. The lighthouse was tall and white like a swirly whipped vanilla ice-cream cone sticking up out of the sea. That is, if swirly whipped vanilla ice-cream cones had giant lights at the top of them. It jutted out into the bay so the water lapped against it.

Mark sat slumped in the back of the car behind us, flicking through *Evil Scientist* magazine. This month's cover feature was called "How to Take Over the World in Ten Easy Steps."

He had his earbuds in and didn't even look up when Dad spoke.

"It's awesome, Mark. An actual lighthouse," I said to him.

Mark shot me an evil glare. "There is nothing awesome about this moron-fest vacation." He pulled his hood up over his head. "You losers have made this the lamest trip ever."

The cooler that was under Sami's feet started shaking. I lifted the lid to investigate. The eyes of Frankie, my zombie goldfish, glowed green as he batted cans of Coke against the sides of the cooler with his fins. He must have heard Mark's voice and gone all zombie mega-thrash fish. He still held a grudge against my brother for trying to murder him with his Evil Scientist toxic gunk. Luckily, Pradeep and I shocked Frankie back to life with a battery, and ever since, he's been our friend and fishy bodyguard. I hoped Frankie would calm down soon.

"Swishy fish!" Sami shouted.

I put my finger to my lips and turned to Sami. "Shhhhhh!"

"What was that, precious?" asked Pradeep's dad.

"Uh, I think she's just excited about seeing fish in the sea," I said, covering for her.

Sami giggled and I carefully closed the lid of the cooler. Safe for now.

As Pradeep and I looked out the window, we saw a thick layer of fog hanging over the lighthouse, wrapping itself around a barely visible sign. I squinted to read it. WELCOME TO EEL BAY, it said in big letters, and then in smaller print that looked like it was painted on just yesterday, DON'T FEED THE EELS! ESPECIALLY THE EVIL ONE!